E H S

EXPLODING HEAD SYNDROME
A MIND MYSTERY

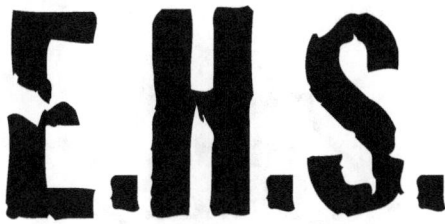

E.H.S.

EXPLODING HEAD SYNDROME
A MIND MYSTERY

P. A. MATTHEW

TRAVEL GRAVEL
MYSTERY SERIES

TRAVEL GRAVEL
MYSTERY SERIES
WHETHER TRAVELING BY FOOT OR BY ARMCHAIR,
TRAVEL BY MYSTERY

Copyright © 2016 Phyllis Mazzocchi
All rights reserved.
No part of this book may be reproduced in any form by any
electronic or mechanical means (including photocopying,
recording, or information storage and retrieval) without permission
in writing from the publisher.

Travel Gravel, 6922 Paseo Del Serra, Los Angeles, CA 90068
www.travelgravel.com
ISBN: 0985521864
ISBN-13: 978-0-9855218-6-8

This book is a work of fiction. Names, characters, places and incidents are products of the author's imagination or are used fictitiously. Any resemblance to actual events, locales, or persons, living or dead, is entirely coincidental. With respect to clinical matters noted in this book, this fictitious story is not intended as a substitute for the medical advice of physicians. The reader should regularly consult with a doctor or other healthcare professional in matters relating to his/her health and particularly with respect to any symptoms that may require diagnosis or medical attention.

ONE

It wasn't the first time that Maggie Bran had seen the orange leaves of autumn make their annual appearance in Poulsbo, but it sure felt like it. Today was a new day. No more hospitals, no more needles, no more analyst's couch. To be behind the wheel of her Jeep Cherokee with the top down and feel the Pacific Northwest air sweep through her hair was liberation personified.

Maggie threw her head back in a sigh of relief and took a long deep breath, brushing away her tight red curls as they bounced across her eyes. It felt good to be alive and it felt even better to be going home again. The row of Washington pines that lined the highway were as tall and emerald green as she remembered them, casting a ripple of shadows across the road as she sped by. She smiled with admiration at their ageless beauty. She even let herself imagine they had waited all this time for her return. But the smile on her face sobered down as quickly as it had risen when her thoughts harkened back to a conversation earlier that morning.

"There's no such thing as *Exploding Head Syndrome*," Dr. Caprio had told her. "It's a myth, a fable. It doesn't exist." He had been so adamant about his position.

"The colors, the sounds, the headaches—it's all stress related," he said. For Maggie, medical science held no logical explanation for the explosions of color and noise that had plagued her since childhood.

Dr Caprio leaned forward in his chair, tapping his fingers as if there were invisible piano keys on the desk in what any other psychologist probably would have labeled as anxiety behavior. He was a kind man who was truly interested in his patients, but sometimes Dr. Caprio could take on the persona of a basketball coach edging his patients onwards to victory. Along with his doctoral degree and professional awards, the wall behind him was plastered with autographed photos of the Seattle Sonics.

His boyish smile curled up at one edge as he stroked the top of his thinning brown hair. Dr. Caprio leaned forward and softened his voice in a gesture of intimacy. "Don't think so hard. Just relax and clear your mind," he chided. Do the visualization techniques, just the way we practiced, okay?"

Maggie lowered her eyes and nodded in acquiescence. She attempted a brave front, but inside she felt frail and afraid. Although she could remember nothing about her mother's death in a boating accident when she was eight years old, Maggie had shortly afterwards become sensitive to an inexplicable stress phenomenon that remained with her all her life. It would begin with a sudden onslaught of noise—an excruciating roar of metallic-like clatter that charged her head; rapidly followed by a fog of pure white light clouding her eyes until she could not see. As in every case of the syndrome, the light of fog would soon transpose into a sea of blackness where blue and yellow sparks flickered and whirled until they burst into little "explosions" of color pulsating through her brain.

Maggie researched far and wide in an effort to find similar documentation of her experience in Western medical journals and patient studies. Among the endless papers written on the physiology of the brain, the mysteries of mind and the consequences of extreme stress, some progressive thinkers had named such an episode "Exploding Head Syndrome." Was it the misfiring of neurons, an emotionally induced hallucination or something else entirely? No one really knew. To Maggie's dismay, conventional science did not acknowledge or treat any such phenomenon as *Exploding Head Syndrome*. In the fields of neurology and psychology, it just didn't exist on paper.

After what most people would term a breakdown, Maggie arrived at Woodsbury House for treatment and rest. The "problem" that had lain dormant for ten years was exacerbated by the stress of her divorce, and now, after nine months of intensive therapy, Dr. Caprio deemed her ready to go it alone.

"We've been through the worst of it together Maggie, and after all this time, I have confidence that you know what to do."

His tone was calming as he reassured her. "You're gonna make it. Really you are. You'll find the steady ground you're looking for, and when you find it, you'll build your confidence again. You'll put the pieces of your life together. I know you will."

Dr Caprio sat upright against the back of his chair and folded his arms together with a slap. "After all, you're one of my best pupils. I always recognize a winner when I see one!"

Maggie gave a nervous laugh as she glanced past his shoulder at the wall. She couldn't help but notice the photograph of Dr. Caprio, arm in arm with his college basketball team.

TWO

Some things never changed in Poulsbo and that was for the best. The historic downtown of the city coined "Little Norway" by its Scandinavian founders dated clear back to the 1800s. Located on the northern end of the Kitsap Peninsula, its fjord-like setting offered spectacular vistas of the Olympic Mountains and Liberty Bay, inspiring its original settlers to model the town center in the likeness of a Norwegian village.

"Velkommen til Poulsbo" (*Welcome to Poulsbo*) the mural beckoned.

Maggie made a sharp turn off the roadway past the quaint streets of colorful storefronts, many of them embellished with ornately hand-painted signs. Both a facsimile of a time gone by and a beloved home to many, the old-world charm of Poulsbo didn't wreak of the commercialization that could have made it untenable for the average person to live in. While its main street sported the picturesque touches of a clock tower and steeple church, its pine-spiked slopes were unobtrusively terraced with modest homes. The conveniences of a grocery store, laundromat, and pharmacy interlaced the souvenir shops, galleries, and restaurants—all traces of the suburban community that resided behind its faux veneer. Maggie had

5

always been drawn to Poulsbo in spite of its play-town ambience.

"Annual Clearance Sale"—the sign above Grimwald's Antique Store caught Maggie's eye. How she loved rummaging through heirlooms, and over the years finding untold treasures in her travels, including a cloisonné vase from China, a nineteenth century stone lithograph, and a one-of-a-kind art deco ring. As a photographer, she was always on the lookout to add to her collection of vintage cameras.

Maggie felt her energy rise as she pulled into a parking space and leapt out the car. The ordinary act of stopping at a rummage sale brightened her mood and almost made her feel like her old self again. Besides, maybe she could pick up something for her new apartment, she justified to herself.

Galloping down the stairway to the basement level entrance with the prance of a spirited pony, she suddenly halted with a scare. "Aah!" she yelped aloud as her heart gave a start. What she had mistaken for a statue had suddenly moved! Maggie clutched her hand to her chest in spontaneous reflex, as the towering figure of a Norwegian farmer, dressed in full ancestral costume, tipped his straw hat. "Good morning, Madame," he said. Maggie sprung backwards on her heel, losing her balance for a brief moment. The guy gave her the creeps, just standing there motionless with his glassy unblinking eyes staring into nowhere.

He was a large beefy man, over six feet in height, with scrappy blond hair that hung down to his chin in uneven layers. His denim jumpsuit was buckled with a pair of suspenders embroidered in the flowery Norwegian design called rosemale, and in his closed fist, he held a farmer's pitchfork. Maggie walked passed him in a huff, not responding to his greeting. It was a small fright, and silly, she knew, but nevertheless it was a fright and the first one she'd experienced since leaving Woodsbury.

"Maggie, I haven't seen you in ages!" Mr. Grimwald met her with outstretched arms as she swung through the door. Always with an ear-to-ear smile, the apron-clad Mr. Grimwald embraced her with a bear hug, awkwardly bumping his gold-rimmed glasses into her shoulder in the process. "Where have you been?"

"I've been, uh . . . on assignment, a photography assignment for a new magazine."

Mr. Grimwald leaned back to take a better look at her. "My goodness, Maggie. You are a sight for my poor old aging eyes."

"Who's the new mannequin?" she asked, still shaken from the incident at the front door.

"Oh, new guy, calls himself Lars. Been here a month or so. Wish I had hair like that, eh?" He bellowed a hearty cackle as he patted his balding head in self-effacing humor.

But by then Maggie was only half listening to Mr. Grimwald as she moved through the shop exploring display tables teeming with porcelain plates, picture frames, clocks, and an assortment of potpourri, all haphazardly placed in no particular order. She singled out a book from the yard-high stack on the window bench and flipped her thumb through its pages.

"Still looking for that first edition Robert Frost, eh?"

Maggie blushed. Robert Frost had been a favorite poet of her ex-husband, Brett, and Mr. Grimwald knew it.

"Actually, I thought I'd find something for my new apartment," she said, quickly changing the subject.

"New apartment?"

"Yes, imagine that—after all these years of driving down from Everett to visit Poulsbo as a tourist, I've finally decided to move here. I'm renting a loft just over the harbor."

"Well, my dear, this is great news. Just got in some new merchandise that might fill the bill for that new apartment of yours—follow me!" He led Maggie to the back of the store, causing her to break into a smile as he knocked into the corner of a table as he walked by. Notorious for his clumsiness, Mr. Grimwald was affectionately known as a bit of a bull in a China shop to his friends.

"Estate Sale—local fella—a widower selling everything," he said, pointing to a dozen or so boxes as yet to be unpacked.

"What happened to his wife?"

"Don't know, but they seemed to be a well-stocked couple by the looks of it." Reaching deep into the first box, he retrieved a banker's lamp, vintage toaster, and an old Leica M3 camera. "He was mighty anxious to let go of the past and move on, though. Got all this for a pittance. But I shouldn't be telling *you* that," he chortled, realizing that he had just forfeited his bargaining leverage.

The front doorbell rang out in a jingle-jangle, sounding exactly like a set of Christmas bells as a handful of customers spilled into the store. Mr. Grimwald grabbed a matte-knife from his hip pocket and sliced open the rest of the cardboard boxes for Maggie's inspection, then turned his attention to the teenage patrons meandering through his store. "You take your time and have fun looking through these boxes . . . and for what it's worth, Maggie, I'm sorry to hear that you and your hubby split. I always thought you two had something special."

Maggie fidgeted with the buttons on the Leica while not really paying attention to the camera at all. The reference to her ex-husband made her uneasy. She wasn't ready to confront her divorce in social situations. Not yet, anyway. Not until she found that steady ground beneath her feet that Dr. Caprio had spoken of. And for now, that ground was still shaky.

THREE

"Maggie . . . Maggie Bran . . . the photographer," she enunciated each word into the telephone, feigning an air of confidence. "Yes, he knows me. He knows my work." Her shoulders fell into a slump as her frustration grew. On the other end of the line, an unyielding personal assistant blocked her message to a photographer's rep. "Well, please . . . please tell him that I called again and that I'm back in town. I'm ready . . . ready to go on assignment at a moment's notice." Her voice dropped, sensing defeat. "Yes, well, uh, thank you."

Maggie slammed down the phone. For a moment she remained frozen in place, sitting there cross-legged on the wooden floor of her loft, surrounded by piles of cardboard boxes and unpacked luggage. She hated looking for a job. She was just not very good at promoting herself, faking an upbeat voice and trying to make excuses for the reason she left town.

"It's time to take a break," she said aloud, releasing a wheezy sigh of exasperation as she stretched her arms out to relax. She leaned her head back on the edge of the couch and surveyed the white stucco walls of her apartment one at a time. With the slow studied focus of a scientist recording an observation, she mentally decorated the room in her mind; lost in her own thought until a shaft of sunlight streaming through the bay window shifted her attention to the sounds of the harbor outside.

"Such a perfect view!" She opened the tallest of the windows and lifted her chin up to feel the cool sea breeze brush against her face. At dockside below, patrons of Molly's Fish n' Chips chatted while waiting in queue, a group of kids guzzled waffles stuffed with hand-churned ice cream from Mrs. Olsen's bakery, and a few hopeful pelicans held their stance along the pilings; too lazy to fish for themselves but eager to catch a stray morsel from the fishermen's rods as they cast their lines off the pier. Out in the marina, rows of sailboats bobbed in their perch, awaiting their launch into the pewter blue waters of the sound. And just beyond their masts, a solitary figure of a man in a neon-green kayak rowed across the glassy surface of the bay, reflecting a mirror image.

Maggie instantly perceived the layout of a photograph framed in her mind's eye. Her camera . . . where was her camera when she needed it? Remembering that her photo gear was still packed away in the Jeep, she rifled through her shopping bag. There was no time like the present to test the vintage Leica she purchased at Grimwald's. She was a stickler for film anyway, having resisted digital formats for as long as she could.

Unscrewing the leather casing from the camera body, she fumbled to unstick what she thought was a rusty release button, until the obstacle, a scrap of coral print cloth, fell out into her lap. Maggie noticed the strong fragrance right away.

"Hmmm . . . incense . . . maybe sandalwood or patchouli," she pressed her nose closer to take a good whiff, not really able to pin down the scent. The scrap was roughly five inches in length with a distinctive motif of cobalt-blue triangles laid out in circles against a coral red background. Two of the edges were shredded and torn.

Maggie took another sniff. The aroma was strangely delicious, but still, she just couldn't place it. She moved to toss the scrap in the trash, but on second thought, changed her mind. "Makes a good deodorizer, if anything," she mused, and stuffed it into her backpack.

Checking to make certain the kayaker was still within frame, Maggie loaded the Leica with a fresh roll of high-contrast film. The cumulus clouds that stippled the sky had just begun to part, causing radiating beams of light to cross over the horizon. She lifted the rangefinder to her eye and poised to snap a photo at just the right moment. When the sunlight had finally reached its peak, she pressed the shutter button.

"Vroom!" Out of nowhere, a force of power knocked her backwards. She stumbled, catching her elbow on an armchair to break her fall.

"Vroom!" A blast of sound reverberated—a metallic-like noise that crashed like a cymbal in her head. "Oh no, not again! Why is this happening?" she cried aloud, as a pervasive white fog all but obliterated her sight. Was it the EHS again? Was she going insane?

She clasped her fingers to her neck in a defensive grip. The world turned to blackness in an eruption of blue sparks, then red, yellow and green—like an aurora of fireworks exploding in all directions. A feeling of fright reared up her throat in a suffocating choke as what sounded like a distant foghorn mixed in to the raucous clamor. Then, a hand reached out and stretched its fingers towards her. For a split-second, Maggie wasn't certain if it was her own hand, or not.

Maggie dropped the camera and covered her ears. She hurled herself on the bed and buried her face in the pillow. "No, no, no!" Her heart was pounding. She could feel a hot flush of blood rush to the top of her head. Clenching her fists, she pounded the mattress. "Please, not again!"

But Maggie was no stranger to this circumstance. EHS had followed her for most all of her life. As a child, and again as a young woman, she had resigned herself to the fact that she might always have to live with these episodes. In fact, she had carefully devised her own set of tactics to deal with them.

Maggie reached for the CD player on the nightstand and switched it on. The music began with the sweet murmur of a muted trumpet. She hummed along, attempting to recover herself. "Better, now better," she heard Dr. Caprio's voice coaching her like an athlete: "You can do it, Maggie, you can do it."

The melody swept through her body. Her humming grew stronger and more confident. She visualized herself floating on an ocean of undulating waves, buoyant and rocking to and fro until the music steadily transported her to a place that was safe and danger free. Slowly but surely, the nausea lifted from her stomach. Maggie breathed a sigh of relief. She had made it through. It was over.

"Hello, anyone home? Hello?" came a knuckle-rap at the door. A woman's voice called out over the music, catapulting Maggie from the slumber of the trumpet's lullaby.

"It's Joanna . . . Joanna from Apartment 210."

Maggie gave herself a quick check in the mirror and blotted her eyes with a tissue before she opened the door. "Hello, sorry . . . the music was so loud that I . . . "

"I'm Joanna, Joanna from Apartment 210, across the hall." The attractive brunette standing before her had shoulder-length hair folded under in a Veronica Lake-style pageboy. She extended a welcoming handshake. "And this is my son, Josh. Josh, say *hello*." A freckle-faced boy with a bowl-shaped Beatle-cut, not more than six years old, hid behind her back and anxiously tugged at his mother's shirt.

"Maggie Bran. So nice to meet you. Please excuse the mess in here. I'm still unpacking."

14

"Oh, not to worry—after all, you just moved in. Welcome to Harbor View Apartments. I've brought you a little something from Mrs. Olsen's Bakery." Joanna presented Maggie with a freshly baked coffeecake, still steaming from the morning's oven.

"Why, thank you. Apricot, it's my favorite . . . really."

"Josh, Josh leave that alone!" Joanna yelled, as Josh, an electronics whiz kid, made his way into Maggie's apartment and zeroed in on her laptop. "This is so cool," he squealed!

"It's okay, really, I don't mind. He probably knows how to use it much better than I do," said Maggie.

Joanna sensed that Maggie needed a little cheering up. "We were just about to have lunch at the harbor. Won't you join us?"

"Oh, but I have so much to do . . . "

"Aw, come on, whatever it is can wait. It's a beautiful day and we're neighbors now—let's get to know each other."

"Yes, yes, come with us!   Mom, make her come with us!" Josh chimed in.

"Okay, it's two against one, and a walk to the harbor does sound like a good idea," Maggie conceded, "Let's go."

FOUR

A light drizzle sprinkled the air. It was just the kind of feathery mist that any resident of Washington State had come to take in stride if they lived there long enough. Maggie paused curbside to dig through the camera equipment packed in her Jeep.

"So, you're a photographer, then?"

"Ah, did I give myself away?" Maggie replied with an embarrassed laugh.

"Every photographer that I know feels naked without a camera."

It was true; Maggie always carried a camera wherever she went and felt lost without one. In some ways, the camera had become her armature against the world, shielding her from direct contact with people and substituting as a pacifier for her anxieties.

Maggie gave the thumbs up as she retrieved one of her digital Nikons. "Got it! Never want to miss that perfect shot."

Josh made a run towards the pier mimicking the sea gulls that squawked overhead as Maggie and Joanna followed behind.

"Josh, hold it down, Josh," Joanna sighed in frustration.

But Maggie took the opportunity to snap away while they chatted. It was another small act that made her feel like her old self again. "Do you know if there's a ferry out of Poulsbo? I thought I heard a foghorn last night," she queried.

"Hmmm, I don't think that's possible. You can catch a ferry from Seattle to Bainbridge Island or from Edmonds, but not to and from Poulsbo. So, I guess that means you're not from this area, then?"

"Actually, I'm a native of Washington State, but originally from Everett. I often visited here with my . . . uh, I mean, I used to come here for weekends now and then. There was always something about Poulsbo that appealed to me."

"There's a pretense about it, don't you think?"

"Excuse me?" Maggie's eyebrows knitted in curious expression.

"Well, I mean, don't you think that in some ways this is a town pretending to be something it's not? After all, we *are* in the Pacific Northwest, *not* Norway."

"I never saw it that way—it *is* an authentic settlement, after all," Maggie reconsidered, "but then, why are you here?"

Joanna's voice shifted. "Circumstances, divorce . . . believe me honey, I'd be riding high in the bright lights of New York City if I had my way. Shared custody—you know how that goes. Josh needs to be close to his Dad."

Maggie took note of Joanna's Armani sunglasses and Kenneth Cole handbag. She wore white Capri pants with a grey angora sweater; her tall slender figure augmented by three-inch spiked heels that seemed misplaced for a casual walk at the harbor. The huge emerald ring on her left hand was impossible to ignore.

"Here we go, best chowder in town." Joanna gestured towards the Norse Harbor Restaurant, an open-gallery post and beam structure with notched corners and a stave roof reminiscent of medieval Norwegian architecture. A miniature replica of a Viking longship dangled at the entry.

"Mom, can I get fish sticks?" wailed Josh.

"Fish sticks, it is. One order of fish sticks, two chowders and three lemonades," Joanna looked to Maggie for agreement as she placed an order at the counter. "So how about you, ever been married?"

Maggie diverted attention to the nearby picnic tables, sprinting ahead to claim one. She planted a #17 plastic marker to the only unoccupied table as if it were a stake into the ground.

Joanna noticed the obvious deflection. "Oh, sorry. I didn't mean to intrude," she said apologetically.

"No, no, it's okay," said Maggie, knowing full well that she didn't want to disturb that part of herself yet. When she resumed her sentence, she emphasized each word as if speaking in a foreign language for the first time: "Yes, I was married. It didn't work out. I came here to start over. Poulsbo is a new start for me."

"You still love him, don't you?"

Maggie looked overhead towards the soda bar. She didn't answer.

"Well, no love lost between me and my ex," said Joanna. "But, I do know what it's like to start over."

"Good afternoon ladies, I'm your server Johann." The conversation halted as the waiter arrived with their food. "That's one order of fish sticks, two chowders, and three lemonades," he said, placing their order on the table and removing the #17 marker. Maggie noted that "Johann" wore a black Norwegian *bunad*, a short double-breasted jacket with gold buttons that was paired with a knee-length pant. His multi-colored vest and white stockings completed the picture of a Norwegian gentleman in his Sunday best. In fact, with his blond hair and toothy grin, Maggie couldn't help but think that he looked straight out of "Hollywood Central Casting." For a split second, his piercing blue eyes fixed onto hers. He seemed to throw her a smirk, but she wasn't sure.

"Hey, if you're looking for a job, I think I can help," said Joanna, breaking Maggie's spell of thought. "My ex-husband's brother runs *Travel Arts Magazine*, based right here in town. They always need good photographers. Interested?"

"Interested?" Maggie's mood lightened. "Joanna, you're a godsend."

"Great, his name is Scott Simon. I'll tell him about you. Give me your number and if he's got something, I'll have him call you."

Maggie jotted her phone number on a napkin and handed it to Joanna, but all the while her eyes were tracing the waiter as he walked behind the counter and whispered into the ear of a hostess.

As her eyes zoomed in on his mouth, she could not resist the compulsion. She found herself trying to read his lips.

FIVE

The Blue Mosque in Istanbul, the rugged sea stacks of Galway Bay, the cobble-stone village of Éze on the French Riviera . . . Maggie perused the oversized framed photos as she hung them on the wall. A purist in the most traditional sense when it came to photography, her favorite medium was still film. While most job assignments called for the expediency of the digital format, Maggie had stubbornly held on to her old darkroom equipment. There was still something magic about the beam of light filtering through a lens and transforming the silver emulsion on a piece of beautifully textured paper. To her mind, it was the format of black and white film that captured the raw honesty of her most precious travel moments like none other. And maybe, it was those early memories of standing alongside her mother, anticipating the emergence of an image coming to life in the developer tray that enhanced the sense of magic. Just she and her mom, quiet and alone in the blackness of a darkroom; the sound of the timer ticking, the red light of the safety bulb— such indelible memories they were. Maggie straightened the corners of the white frames so they lined up to perfection. Their placement opposite the bay window was ideal to catch the full light of day.

It was 10pm, so she was startled when the phone rang. "Hello, Maggie Bran here."

"Hi there Maggie, it's Scott . . . Scott Simon from Travel Arts Magazine. Sorry to call you so late, but Joanna didn't think you'd mind."

"Oh, no problem. She's right, I don't mind. I'm a night owl at heart."

"Well, me too—hey, that could come in handy sometime! Maggie, I was wondering if you could meet me in my office tomorrow morning. I think I've got a great assignment for you."

"Of course I can . . . can't wait to hear about it . . . say 9am?"

"9am it is. I'm on Liberty Bay Drive, just above the tackle shop. Oh, and Maggie . . . let's just say I hope you have your passport ready."

"Oh, it's ready. It's always ready Mr. Simon. See you tomorrow . . . and thank you, thank you very much for calling."

Maggie looked up to the proverbial heavens in grateful gesture. Maybe her new start was about to begin, after all. Grabbing a shawl, she climbed the rooftop ladder to the terrace above her loft to get some fresh air. A white haze of fog riddled the sky so there were no stars to be seen, but the chill of night felt invigorating. She squeezed her arms across her chest and nuzzled the shawl closer to her neck. She both loved the fog and hated it. In some ways it was a metaphor for the obfuscation of childhood memories she could not tap—and in other ways, it made her feel close to something important she could not define.

Maggie thought back to the frightening episode earlier that day. She heard the voice of Dr. Caprio echo once again: "Your problem is that you think too hard, Maggie." She knew it was true. Sometimes she thought so hard that she questioned her own judgment, second-guessing herself into missteps, and even divorce. What ever became of the unfettered instincts that never failed her as a child, she wondered, recalling another foggy night when on a holiday trip to Italy with her parents, she had been undaunted by the maze of cryptic alleyways that befuddled most tourists in Venice. "How do you know which way to go?" asked her Dad, amazed at her ability to lead the family out from the winding labyrinth of narrow streets to the Piazza San Marco. "I just know Dad, I just know . . ."

A foghorn sounded in the distance . . . or at least, she thought it was a foghorn, but how could that be? Maggie shivered as her arms tensed up. The blare of a foghorn scared her, but she didn't know why. Fear and intuition were all rolled up into one big ball, and she could no longer distinguish between the two. Nothing was as it seemed. According to Joanna, not even the town she lived in was real . . . and yet she was drawn to it, like the fog.

SIX

"Have a seat. Scott will be right with you," gushed the perky tee-shirt and jean-clad receptionist. To Maggie, it felt more like she was in a television newsroom than a magazine headquarters. The office was outfitted with six monitors, each of them tuned to a different cable station: CNN, Discovery, The History Channel, National Geographic, the Style Network, and even HGTV. A line of digital clocks were labeled and arranged in a neat column down the wall, concurrently flashing the times in New York, London, Paris, Istanbul, and Tangier. Behind her, the office buzzed with a charge of electricity; voices shouting over cubicle walls, boxes arriving via parcel post, and a pack of hungry customers assailing the Breakfast Basket vendor. "Any plain bagels, today?" someone yelled. "Anyone got change of a twenty?"

Maggie felt a whoosh of air at her back as a blur of a figure whizzed by, took a seat, and swiveled around to face her, all in a matter of seconds. "Hi, I'm Scott," he said, offering his hand out for a shake.

Maggie was thunderstruck at how handsome he was. His thick, black hair was slicked under in a debonair wave reminiscent of a swashbuckling Errol Flynn. A thin tapered mustache framed his

24

dimpled smile, and a pair of arched eyebrows capped the searing dark eyes that locked into hers. He smacked of the flamboyant charm of Hollywood's most notorious lady-killer.

Releasing his hand, Maggie remained fixed on the pool of his large brown eyes. He smiled back at her as if he had just discovered a trove of gold. His eyes scaled down her chest.

"Nice to meet you," she responded with a blush. She glanced down at his left hand. He wasn't wearing a ring.

"Well, Maggie, you may not know me, but I know *you*."

Maggie was taken aback.

"I've been looking at your work," he explained, turning to his laptop and scrolling the page of photographs on Maggie's wEHSite. "I can tell by your attention to detail that you'd be perfect for the job."

"Well great, that's great. I can't wait to hear about it. What's the assignment?"

Scott slid a folder of printouts in front of her and slapped his hand on the desk for emphasis. "Textiles!"

"Pardon me?"

"Textiles, but not just any textiles—Moroccan textiles," he said, as he resumed scrolling the photographs. "Travel Arts Magazine, we specialize in travel, themed in art. You know, touring Rome to see the Caravaggio paintings, Barcelona for the Gaudy architecture, or Crete for the Minoan artifacts. We have endless ideas for themes. Art is everywhere, wouldn't you agree?" He spun around in his chair and gave her a flirty smile. "Kind of like you," his tone shifted an octave lower, "classic Botticelli with that curly red hair and ivory skin—now *there's* a work of art."

Maggie straightened her shoulders, fingering a strand of hair behind her ear in a gesture of self-consciousness. Scott Simon was certainly living up to his movie star image.

"So, are you interested?" His eyes sparkled seductively.

"Uh, in the assignment—yes, yes of course," answered Maggie. She could feel her face turn pink with blush.

"Great, you leave in two days for Marrakech. An associate of mine will meet you there. He'll write the story, you'll take the photographs."

A buzzer interrupted, prompting Scott to pick up the line. "Sorry, gotta take this call," his speech accelerated, "my assistant will make your travel arrangements and fax you all the details. Thanks so much for coming. I know you'll do a great job." He stood for a parting handshake.

"I won't let you down," said Maggie, releasing her hand as she backed out slowly. But when the door slammed behind her, she could no longer contain her excitement. Morocco, she was going to Morocco! Bolting down the steps with the excitement of a child on Christmas day, she nearly bumped into a fisherman toting bait from the tackle shop. Visions of an exotic Kasbah danced in her head—what to wear, what to pack—and research, she would need to do lots of research! Her mind was racing with plans when she heard the one voice that she would recognize anywhere.

"Hello, Maggie." For a moment, her breath stilled. The sight of his tousled brown hair, day-old beard, and the familiar broad shoulders that she once loved to fall into, brought a sting of pain. It was her ex-husband, Brett standing right there in front of her on the boardwalk.

"Hi, what brings you to Poulsbo?" She felt her voice become a whimper. He could still make her knees weak.

He came closer, his hands dug into the pockets of his overcoat. "I'm here for the weekend," he said.

The pause between them was palpable when Maggie stuttered: "Are you . . . are you with someone?" She wondered if he would ever have brought another woman to their special place.

Brett motioned his head left to right, indicating the negative. "No, no Maggie. I'm here alone." His mood became upbeat when he continued, "I'm here to look at real estate."

"Real estate?"

"Yes, I'm surveying an investment property on the other side of the harbor. Just here for the day." He shuffled on his feet. "And you Maggie, how are you?"

"Great!" she answered in an exaggerated burst of energy. "Just great. In fact, I leave for Morocco in two days."

"Wow, Morocco. Congratulations!" He looked genuinely happy for her, but the obvious distance between them kindled a twinge of sadness. Time had passed, yet there was still so much she didn't understand. Why hadn't he stood by her when she was ill? Why hadn't he fought harder for her? She wished he would suggest they grab a cup of coffee, but she knew that he wouldn't.

Brett looked down at his wristwatch. "Well, gotta get going. Good luck, Maggie. Take care of yourself in Morocco. Nice seeing you."

"Nice seeing you too, Brett," she said, feigning her best smile.

SEVEN

"I wanna help!" squealed Josh, about to run through the open door of Maggie's apartment. Joanna caught him by the shirt collar, just in time.

"Maggie, Maggie it's Joanna!" she called out from the portal of the doorway. Two suitcases were already in the hall, packed and ready to go.

Maggie emerged breathless from the bedroom. "Oh Joanna—hi, I meant to call you. Guess what?"

"Ah yes, I already know. I heard the good news from Scott—you're leaving for Morocco today. I came to help out with the packing." Josh wriggled his collar from his mother's grip and sprinted to the camera equipment on the table.

"Josh, do *not* touch those cameras. Those are not toys," said Joanna sternly.

Maggie noticed the book in Joanna's hands. "What's this?"

"It's a gift, a gift for your trip—the seminal book on Moroccan textiles."

The gesture was a surprise. "Well, thank you. How thoughtful of you." Maggie flipped through a few pages at random.

"Colors, threads, weaves, everything you need to know about Moroccan textiles and more. You'll want to take that with you," said Joanna.

Over on the sofa, Josh played with Maggie's equipment, packing and unpacking the cameras from her backpack.

"Josh, you stop that right now!" Joanna turned to Maggie apologetically. "I'm so sorry, Maggie. I'll put everything back."

"I wanna help, too," Josh whined.

"You can help by keeping hands off," scolded Joanna.

But Maggie was unconcerned. She was preoccupied with the more pressing business of reviewing her traveler's checklist. "Just a few more things to check off the list," she yelled from the kitchen, as she methodically crossed off each item on a list of "things to do" before she locked up the house.

"Done!" she declared aloud, as she set the automatic light timer, and checked it off the list.

"Done!" she proclaimed as she switched off the fan.

Lowering the blinds was the next "to do" on the list, but as Maggie tugged at the cord of the big bay window, she hit upon a knot. She paused to untangle it and casually looked outside. Standing there on the street corner and leaning against a lamppost was a man who looked oddly familiar. She almost didn't recognize him without his uniform. The large build, the scraggly blond hair—could it be Lars, the costumed Norwegian farmer from Grimwald's Antique Store? And what was he doing there, anyway?

"Maggie, is anything wrong?" shouted Joanna.

"No, no problem, just a knot in the pull cord. Be right there," Maggie replied. She was spooked by the unsettling sight of Lars beneath her window, but just shrugged it off and closed the blinds. "All Done!"

Joanna and Maggie carried the first of the luggage downstairs to the awaiting taxi—but alone inside the apartment, Josh was still intent on helping out. Spotting the vintage Leica that Maggie purchased at Grimwald's displayed in a bookcase like a decorative knickknack, he was certain she had forgotten it. Snatching the camera off the shelf, he shoved it to the bottom of her backpack and zipped it in. Maggie would be so pleased when she found it there.

"Done!" he pronounced.

EIGHT

Maggie was unprepared for just how beautiful Marrakech would be. From the minute she stepped off the airplane at Menara International Airport, any preconceived notions she had about Morocco were instantly broken.

A mixture of modern style and traditional Moroccan aesthetic, the streets were wide and generous, interlaced with sumptuous gardens of exotic flowers. Predominating the architecture were the dusty rose briquettes mined from the abundance of iron deposits in the nearby Atlas Mountains that earned Marrakech its nickname of the "Red City." Maggie took notice that the native bougainvillea, jacaranda, jasmine, hibiscus, and even cactus, were meticulously cared for and flourishing in the high desert climate.

A camel reclining on a street corner, basked in the afternoon sun, reminding Maggie that she was a Westerner in an exotic culture. Indeed, despite its history of French colonialism, Marrakech had maintained the integrity of its indigenous Berber and Arab heritage, as demonstrated by the Moroccan women in traditional headscarves and floor-length caftans mixed in amongst the tourists sporting shorts and chatting on cell phones.

Maggie spotted the ramparts of the medina and recognized that she was approaching the oldest and most labyrinthine part of the city where the infamous *Djemaa el Fna Square* was located. Her taxi stopped just short of the city walls. "Your hotel, Madame," said the driver.

As Maggie stepped out from the car, her first impression was marked with a "wow!" She had not anticipated such decadence in Scott's choice of hotel. A triple-tiered fountain that could have been mistaken for a giant wedding cake showered cascades of sparkling water in a choreographed display; the precursor to a grand entryway of arched colonnades.

A doorman in a rose-pink uniform tipped his hat and held open the door as two bellboys whisked away her luggage to the hotel lobby that might be described as near garish in its splendor. The vestibule was furnished in an elaborate French Provincial style with walls that were trimmed with Moroccan tiles of blue and gold geometric design. A hotel placard boasted seven dining rooms, two pools, a sauna and even a disco. Judging by the German, French and Spanish accents that caught her ear, Maggie guessed that the luxury hotel was geared towards the creature comforts of the well-heeled. It was a bit too posh for her taste, but was located close to the medina and well within sight of the Koutouba minaret, a famous landmark of the city center.

A message awaited her at the front desk. *"Dear Ms. Bran,"* the handwritten note read, *"I will pick you up for dinner at 8:30 this evening. I look forward to meeting you and discussing our mutual project."* It was signed simply *"Ramos."*

The enormous canopy bed that commanded her luxury suite was draped from ceiling to floor in an ivory French tulle, fastened to the bedposts with satin ribbons, and creating a curtain for the plush cushion of pillows that covered the mattress. Mahogany furniture, a scarlet red Persian rug, and a crystal chandelier comprising dozens of lamps completed the décor.

Maggie skimmed through the fax of instructions from Scott. Her assignment was to photograph and document as many textiles as she could, then upload and email the results each day—but that would begin tomorrow. For now, it was almost dusk and this was not the time for work. This was a time to explore. She reached for her backpack and began to unload equipment. Technically, she had missed a full night of sleep, so she should have felt tired and jet lagged, but as was her modus operandi when traveling, she became energized upon arrival in new surroundings. Her favorite thing to do on the first day in a new city was to wander with no agenda, following a pathless route and feeling her way around by instinct—just like that child in the winding streets of Venice. Of course, she would take a camera with her.

A chamber maid entered the room delivering a stack of fresh towels as Maggie dispersed her cameras and lenses on the coffee table. One at a time, she examined their condition. Sigh! The batteries had all lost their charge, most probably from the air pressure of the long flight. There would be no picture taking tonight.

Maggie plugged in the chargers to let the batteries juice up overnight and carted the backpack to the armoire. "Hmmm, what's this?" She sensed an added weight. Reaching down to the bottom corner of the backpack, she felt a bulky presence. "Ha!" It was none other than the vintage Leica she had purchased at Grimwald's. She couldn't help but laugh aloud. "That's gotta be Josh. Josh, you really did help after all!" There was no charging necessary for this totally manual camera.

"Film, I love film anyway," she muttered, snatching her sunglasses to make a run out the door before nightfall. But as she turned to give her luxury suite a parting once-over, she noticed the chamber maid slumped over and holding her stomach. The folded towels had fallen to the floor.

"Vous étes malade?" (*Are you ill?*) Maggie inquired in French, not knowing any Arabic or Berber. There was no response. Realizing that the chamber maid might not understand either English or French, she motioned for her to sit down, but the young woman held her hand up in a halting gesture and shook her head in refusal. Maggie was concerned. The woman was about twenty years old, pretty, olive-skinned, with her thick black hair tied away from her face in a ponytail, enhancing her youthful stature. Clearly, she was ill, but rules of conduct took precedence over her malady. To take a seat in the chambers of a hotel patron would have been considered inappropriate, and she knew it.

Maggie poured a glass of water and offered it to her, but the woman turned away. The very thought that she was trained to keep her place, such as it was in her world, caused Maggie to feel a swell of empathy. "We are no different," she mouthed silently, but she was powerless under the circumstances and could only offer a warm smile to the young woman in simpatico. The woman smiled back in like kind, as if she understood.

"Good Night," said Maggie gently, and she exited the room.

NINE

"How many camels for you?" From the moment she stepped foot on the pavement, she was inundated by street hustlers. One even offered to take her home. "How many camels for you?" recanted a persistent stalker, as he trailed at her heels. Maggie deadpanned it, not acknowledging the man dressed in a tan djellaba robe. She crossed the avenue and zig-zagged unpredictably in an attempt to shake him off, but to no avail. Her curly red hair was a novelty in Morocco and drew attention.

From a distance, a steady drumbeat pounded. She used it like radar, following its sound until it grew louder and like a magnet led her away from the hotel district and its hustlers to the Djemaa el Fna, an enormous plaza within the old city walls that was notorious for its carnival-like atmosphere.

By now, the beating drum had escalated to a commotion, resembling a barrage of pots and pans crashing together and merging with the shrill fevered pitch of a snake charmer's horn. Maggie joined the crowd of onlookers who gathered in fascination as the turban-headed charmer sat cross-legged on the ground, enticing his serpentine partner from it's basket. A deep sense of calm washed over her—the calm that comes when a traveler has crossed the threshold of one realm in exchange for another. In that moment, not only had she left behind the modernity of the hotel quarter for the adventure of antiquity but she had left behind her old life as well.

A trio of acrobats rolled past her like tumbleweeds. A medicine man weighed his cures on an apothecary scale. Storytellers sold their tales for the price of a coin, and a henna artist painted whirling brown patterns on the hands of a child. Maggie munched contentedly on a slice of fresh coconut and sampled the spicy grilled shish-kebab. She barely knew what to look at first. "Your fortune, today?" beckoned a palm reader.

At the north side of the square, the spectacle of a sinewy fire-eater was attracting an audience. The bare-chested man yelled out to the crowd, rallying their screams for encouragement as he tousled a fire lit torch into the air, then handily caught it on its way back down. A burst of spontaneous applause goaded him on while he teasingly directed the flame towards his mouth in a slow-motion gesture. As the flickering fireball approached his tongue, the anticipation of what was to come intensified to high drama—then in the blink of an eye, it was all over as he swallowed the flame and extinguished it down his throat. The crowd erupted—hooting, hollering, and shouting for more, but for Maggie, it was a relief. She had been so wound up by the death-defying display that she had not once raised her camera to snap a photo. Only now did she position the Leica for the perfect frame.

As the intrepid fire-eater prepared to repeat his daring feat for the second time, blue and yellow sparks sprayed like fireworks from the swirling torch. Maggie wiped the sweat from her forehead and patted her face dry with a tissue. Even at dusk, the air was sizzling, exacerbated by her proximity to the heat of the fire pit.

She winced and rubbed her eyes. Billows of white smoke rose skywards carrying the fragrant scent of exotic spices in their wake, and for a moment blurring her vision. Maggie peered through the viewfinder to capture a shot just as the poker was about to enter the mouth of the fire-eater. Then, she pressed down on the shutter.

"*Vroom!*" A flash of white light clouded her sight. Maggie dug her fists into her eyes. Her ears felt red-hot. "It's the smoke, the heat of the fire," she told herself. Then suddenly, a shock of electricity jolted her body. She stumbled out from the crowd, attempting to get some air, but it was too late. She fell hard to the ground.

The sound of the snake charmer's horn grew sharper and louder until it snowballed to a roar. The beating of the drums grew raucous and brassy; their monotonous tone now a menace to her ears. Maggie thought she saw a woman's face coming towards her through the white fog of smoke, but she wasn't sure. She felt her heart pounding through her chest. A hot sweat of nausea hit her in the gut. Then, just like the scatterings of the fire-eater's torch, a burst of colored sparks exploded in her head—first blue, then yellow, then red. One after another, they repeated in rapid fire—blue, green, red, yellow like a denotation of explosions going off in her head. A hand reached out to her, maybe from the crowd—its fingers stretching, then spinning, circling and melting into tiny eruptions of color — until finally, a dark void of blackness obliterated her sight.

When it was over, an elderly woman was cradling her, holding a vial of perfume under her nose. Maggie recognized her as the fortune-teller who had offered to read her palm. The old woman held her face close to Maggie's, her heavy lidded eyes staring directly into hers. A white kerchief framed her leathered skin and the stringy grey hair that hanged over her brow. Her hands were adorned with rings of purple gemstones on every finger; their facets glistening through the light of the firepit.

"Puzzle," the woman mumbled under her breath, chanting what sounded like a lullaby. Maggie followed the melody note by note, and let it soothe her. *"A puzzle,"* she thought she heard the old woman repeat, as she smeared a drop of oil on Maggie's lip and massaged it in gently. The sugary scent was delectable and strangely familiar.

An audience of onlookers clustered around them as if they were the latest spectacle of the evening. Embarrassed, Maggie shot up from the ground, brushed off her bottom and snatched her camera. "Thank you . . . uh, merci beaucoup, Madame," she stammered to the fortune teller, then ran in the direction of the hotel, following the lights of the Koutouba minaret.

TEN

Ramos arrived right on schedule. When the desk clerk rang her room at 8:30pm, Maggie had just enough time to shower and change clothes. She chose a long flowered skirt and a white peasant blouse covered by a pink cashmere wrap. A last minute pin fastened her still damp hair into a knot of red curls.

Maggie paused in front of the mirror and took a long deep breath to compose herself, then rushed downstairs to the hotel lobby.

"Bon Soir, Madame Bran," the tall, brown-skinned man reached out his hand to shake hers. "I recognize you by your red hair."

"Ah yes, the red hair . . . but please, by all means call me Maggie."

"And please, call me Ramos," he countered, in an accent she could not pinpoint. Sensing her question, he volunteered: "My mother was Berber and my father from Spain, the Costa del Sol."

"Then you come from the best of both worlds," she laughed.

"Yes, and I was educated at your Columbia University in New York. So you might say that I have the best of *many* worlds," he replied with a smile.

Ramos was not what she expected. He was dressed in the traditional Moroccan garb of a djellaba robe, but his American jeans were clearly visible at the hem. An embroidered cap of black and gold threads covered whatever hair he may have had, and a pair of frameless spectacles teetered on the edge of his nose, prompting him to adjust them frequently. He was a man who smiled easily, good-humored and relaxed. He had a composure about him that made everything seem alright with the world, and she liked him instantly.

A short ride in a petit taxi took them behind the medina walls to the lavish grounds of a restaurant housed in the courtyard of a converted eighteenth century palace. Maggie was in awe at first sight of it. "I am certainly not in Poulsbo, anymore," she chuckled to herself.

A gallery of Moorish arches gated with iron latticework, provided a dazzling entré to a series of private rooms where a steward in a white caftan led Ramos and Maggie to the private dining room reserved for them. Bulbous glass fixtures studded with candles hung from the dome of the lofty ceilings, and a cozy fire crackled in the limestone fireplace directly beside their table.

"Please, you do the honors," said Maggie, deferring to Ramos to order a traditional Moroccan meal on her first night in Marrakech.

Speaking in fluent French, he proceeded to order aperitifs, chicken b'stilla; a flaky pastry wrap with ground almonds and spices, couscous, and a tajine stew. "That's a good start," he said jokingly.

Maggie's attention diverted towards the painted ceiling, her eyes surveying the intricate filigree carvings.

"You observe with the eye of an artist," Ramos grinned. "You remind me so much of Lily. "

"Lily?"

"Scott's wife, Lily."

Maggie turned wide-eyed with surprise. "I didn't know Scott was married." She distinctly recalled the lack of a wedding ring.

Ramos hesitated, "Well, Scott *was* married. He's a widower. He lost his wife Lily, last year."

"A widower!" It seemed to Maggie that Scott did not have the demeanor of a grieving widower when she met him.

"Lily was a photographer, just like you, and curious just like you—a fantastic woman."

Maggie listened with no comment, waiting to hear more.

"Afterwards . . ." he said delicately, "after Lily was gone, Scott put all his energy into his magazine and his import business.

"Import business?" Maggie continued to be surprised.

"Textiles, Moroccan textiles, specifically."

Maggie realized there was a whole dimension going on here that she was not aware of. Scott was not only a merry widower, but he owned, not merely managed, Travel Arts Magazine and an international business operation, as well.

"So, our assignment," he continued, switching gears, "is shooting textiles for the magazine. You will take the photographs and I will document and write."

"What will you write about?" asked Maggie, as a waiter replenished her glass with wine.

"Believe me, you'd be surprised how much there is to say about textiles. Every textile design has a story and a place connected to it. The colors, the fabrics, the weaves—they're all specific to the tribal region where they originated."

"Fascinating, so then, each night we upload the photographs and specs on a computer and send them to Scott, right?"

"Right. We start tomorrow—at the souks."

"The souks?"

"The souks—the open-air marketplace in the old city. I assure you, you have never experienced a market like this before. It is a maze of winding alleys—easy to get lost, you'll have to stick close to me."

Maggie thought back to the twisting alleyways of Venice. "I bet I could handle it," she beamed.

But Ramos' voice took a serious tone. "I would not recommend it," he articulated emphatically. "It is not safe for a woman alone in the souks."

ELEVEN

It was crack of dawn when Ramos led her to the far north entrance of the souks. Maggie covered her hand over her mouth to stifle a yawn, hoping that he wouldn't notice. She was still exhausted from the events of the evening before. Had it been the heat, the over-excitement of the fire-eaters performance, or the EHS again? Her blackout at the Square both confused and frightened her. Just thinking about it made her head spin all over again.

"Stick close to me," Ramos cautioned, "I need to know you are by my side at all times!" Maggie nodded in agreement, but she was more than a little amused by his demand since she considered herself to be an experienced world traveler.

Stepping into the marketplace was like entering into a maze; the tightly woven labyrinth of narrow passageways made even more claustrophobic by the abundant array of merchandise bulging over tables and protruding from the open-air stalls. Adding to the chaos, a busload of eager tourists had evidently downed an early breakfast in order to arrive early. They flooded the streets like an army of ants, elbowing their way around each other to peruse the merchandise and inciting the shouts of hawkish vendors who competed for their attention.

46

Ramos navigated the complex network of twists and turns like a pro and seemed to know exactly where he was going. Maggie followed at his heel, half-walking and half-skipping to keep up with his rapid pace. She had to admit that one turn looked just like the other.

"Each section is designated for a different brand of commerce and craftsmanship," explained Ramos in professorial style. "These crafts survive for three reasons—because of tourism, because of the hotels and private residents who employ the artists, and because of foreign investors, like Scott, who import the goods."

"*Tap, tap, tap!*" The strike of a hammer signaled the souk of a blacksmith. "We are now passing the Souk Haddadine in the metalworkers quarter," said Ramos. Inside a darkened compartment and shaded from the sun behind a curtain of burlap, an ironworker skillfully plied a stick of wrought iron characteristic of the many gates and terraces that graced Morocco. Maggie could feel the heat of the forge hit her face as she walked by.

"And now, the Souk Siyyaghin, the jeweler's market." The profusion of bangles, rings, and chains made this the most easily identifiable of the souks.

Maggie held her nose. Ahead of them, from the Souk Cherratine, the pungent odor of leather pelts oozed from the tannery stall where nearby babouche makers sewed the flat pointy slippers that were so popular with tourists.

"A sprig of mint might help that," said Ramos, pausing at the apothecary where hundred of jars lined the shelves. A sign in English read *"Magic Spells and Medicine, Made to Order."* Maggie noticed a dried lizard, a desiccated snake, and the carcass of an unrecognizable animal hanging from a rafter. Ramos bargained for a handful of sprigs and handed them to her. "Just break a leaf and inhale whenever you need to," he instructed.

As they inched their way nearer the trendy Dyer's Souk, "otherwise known as the Souk des Teinturiers," Maggie chose one of the two digital cameras strapped around her neck to photograph the sheafs of red and blue wool hung out to dry.

"We are now approaching the Criée Berbère, the Carpet Market, which was once the center of the old slave trade in Marrakech." A wrought iron gate led to a dimly lit plaza where Berber and Persian rugs covered every inch of wall space.

"It's hard to believe this was once a slave market," said Maggie.

"There was an active slave trade here right up until the year of 1912—but now, as you can plainly see, there are only salesmen courting prospective buyers with a glass of mint tea and the art of persuasion," Ramos grinned.

Maggie detected a lingering scent of perfume hanging in the air. It seemed familiar. "What is that absolutely exquisite scent?"

"A compound of orange flowers, saffron and ginger. It signals that we are approaching the Souk

Smarine, the textile market where our work begins."

Befitting of what from appearances may have been the greater part of the marketplace that Maggie had seen so far, a grand white archway loomed overhead. The term "emporium" or "superstore" would have best described what comprised the amalgam of merchandise showcased under a ceiling of latticework that served the dual purpose of providing some shade while permitting shafts of sunlight to enter.

Rows of textiles were neatly organized by color and design, flanking the merchants' doorways while advertising the patterns unique to each compartment of the souk. Zigzags, triangles, stripes, and squares, in every color combination imaginable, were among the variety of motifs that lay ready for purchase in the form of blankets, shawls, wall hangings and curtains. Maggie began photographing right away.

"Let's start with stripes," said Ramos. "The most basic of the Moroccan textiles are flat and woven in stripes. If you look closely, some weaves are tighter than others." Maggie zoomed in closer to shoot the detail. "The lighter weaves are used for blankets and curtains, the tighter ones as rugs for the floor."

Ramos led her to the adjoining stall of multi-colored striped rugs. "These rugs come from Zemmour, an area southeast of Rabat. You may think all stripes are the same, but notice how these stripes are thinner, and how the white bands interlace with the red, black, and gold threads."

"You were right," said Maggie, snapping away, "there is more to learn about textiles than I ever realized."

"Look here," said Ramos, "the Zayan tribes weave rugs similar to the Zemmour. At first glance, they may look alike, but if you examine the threads closely, the handiwork is distinctly more complex."

He moved to the next vendor and thumbed through the weave of a blue and gold fabric. "And here, another example . . . these Glawa materials are made with an unmistakable pile and twine technique. The Glawa are a tribe from the High Atlas Mountains."

Maggie was beginning to get the connection. The weave, the color and the design connoted the tribe and region that produced it.

"Identify the weave and you locate the tribe that created it," said Ramos. "Makes a good theme for Travel Arts Magazine, don't you think?"

"Yes, a great theme." Maggie stopped to check her shots.

"That's a big advantage of a digital camera, is it not?" said Ramos, "Checking to see if you got the shot, I mean."

"Oh yes, it is indeed. But I'm still old-fashioned when it comes to film."

"Ah yes, film. Lily was brilliantly stubborn when it came to film."

Maggie took pause. Ramos' comment made her stop and think . . . Scott was a widower . . . Lily was a photographer . . . the Leica. Was it possible that Scott could have been the widower selling off the boxes of goods at Grimwald's Antique Store in Poulsbo? Could the Leica have belonged to Lily? She fished for an answer.

"Lily didn't happen to own an old Leica camera, did she?"

"Sure did," Ramos said wistfully, "She carried that camera everywhere. Never left home without it. But how did you guess?"

Maggie shrugged her shoulders in a disarming gesture. "Oh, every photographer wants a vintage Leica," she responded. But silently she could not shake the thought that the camera she purchased at Grimwald's just might belong to Lily.

"Look, that's enough textiles for today. Let's get you back to the hotel to upload these photos to Scott. We'll get to the rest tomorrow."

"Sure, sounds good," said Maggie. But inwardly, her mind was working overtime recounting the words of Mr. Grimwald: *"Estate Sale . . . a widower selling everything . . . he was mighty anxious to let go of the past and move on . . . got all this for a pittance."*

TWELVE

Back at the hotel, there was an urgent message from Scott in Poulsbo: *"Maggie, need to see photos. Please send the first results as soon as possible."* What was the big rush, anyway? Maggie laid out her equipment on the bed and made a quick transfer to her laptop, meticulously identifying each photo by name and region using Ramos' notes. When she was done, she heaved a huge sigh of relief. "Whew! Pressure off!"

Exhausted, she fell back on to the canopy bed; the drape of the French tulle hanging about her like a curtain. Massaging her fingers into the burrows of her forehead, she stared into space through the sheer ivory folds. A fusillade of thoughts were swimming in her head . . . Scott . . . Lily . . . the camera.

"Don't think so hard, Maggie." Dr. Caprio's voice replayed. But something was needling her, prodding her, and pushing at her from behind the grind of thoughts. Maggie nestled her head into the plush feathered pillows and explored the white-netted curtain that surrounded her. It was not unlike the curtain of fog she could not see through; for the memories of the past that she could not tap. Had the Exploding Head Syndrome returned? Had something set it off? Maggie mulled over her day at the souks, the sound of the

blacksmith's hammer, the patterns of colorful textiles, the smell of exotic perfume . . .

"That's it!" Maggie shot up from the bed and reached for her backpack. She turned it upside down and shook it out wildly. The scrap of cloth . . . the scented rag that was stuck in the Leica case when she opened it. "Where is it, where is it?" she muttered, emptying every last item out of the bag until finally there it fell, onto the pillow.

She raised the scrap of cloth to the lamps of the chandelier to examine it against the light, noting the distinctive design of cobalt blue triangles interwoven in circles with coral red stripes. From what she had learned from Ramos today, this pattern indicated the origin of its weavers. She held the scrap up to her nose and sniffed it, recollecting her conversation with Ramos back in the souks that morning. *"What is that absolutely delicious aroma?"* she had asked.

"A combination of orange flowers, saffron and ginger. It signals we are approaching the textile souk . . ." he had answered.

The scent was the same! The cloth had meant nothing to her at the time she found it, but now she guessed that it must have come from the textile souk. Maggie glanced out the window. It was still daylight. She took the Leica in hand and stuffed the remnant of cloth into her pocket. She knew what she had to do.

THIRTEEN

When she arrived at the souks, the marketplace was still bustling with the day's commerce. An American tour group had just unloaded from a sightseeing bus and was piling into the maze of alleyways, packing it in like sardines. Maggie was uncertain of which way to turn.

Heat, sound, smell, sight. The heat of the blacksmith's forge, the tapping of the hammer, the smell of the leather tanning, the sight of the colorfully dyed wool. If she could just follow her senses as benchmarks to Ramos' tour, she knew she could find her way.

"*Tap, tap, tap!*" She heard the strike of the blacksmith's hammer. Maggie navigated through the mob, managing to find the first landmark of the Souk Haddadine. She felt the heat of the forge clip her face. She was going in the right direction.

"*Heat, sound, smell, sight,*" Maggie chanted to herself like a mantra. The shimmering bangles of the Jewelry Souk came within sight . . . the acid stench of leather pelts set out to dry at the tannery stall in the Souk Cherratine . . . the vivid colors of the Dyer's souk. The textile market could not be far.

Maggie fondled the camera in the cradle of her hands and tried to imagine Lily. Somehow the Leica was key. It seemed to her that each time she used the camera, at the apartment in Poulsbo and during the fire-eater's performance at the Djemaa el Fna, she had had what felt like an EHS experience. Was it the stress of an event that she was intuiting, just like when her mother died in a boat accident? Was Lily's camera somehow speaking to her? She had to find out.

A party of tourists blocked the pathway ahead. Maggie tightened her arms closer to her chest and squeezed her way through. "So sorry, excuse me," she apologized, as she unavoidably brushed against one gentlemen wearing a Yankees baseball cap.

The scent of orange blossoms signaled that she was approaching the Souk Smarine, and Maggie felt relieved when she recognized the high white arch and trellis that was its entryway. She reached into the pocket of her jeans and retrieved the scrap of cloth. What significance did it have?

Stripes, diamonds, triangles, squares and crosshatched designs were exhibited in every pattern imaginable. From left to right and back again in every direction, it all looked the same. She was surrounded by textiles of every color and design and without the help of Ramos, she couldn't tell the difference between them. She held the Leica in both hands and peered through the viewfinder. Her intuition told her that through the camera, she would know what to do next— but this time, she would continue shooting, no matter what happened.

She pressed the shutter button. *"Vroom!"* A blast of heat knocked her sideways, twisting her ankle, as her heel turned in her shoe.

"Aaah . . ." Maggie reached down to adjust her sandal, momentarily releasing her finger from the shutter. The glare of the afternoon sun filtered through the lattice overhead, shining directly in her eyes, but she fought to regain her balance and re-positioned the camera to frame the next shot. She was determined to keep going.

She pressed down on the shutter for a second time. The filtered beams of sunlight surged into a blinding white light of fog, surrounding her and penetrating her head. Her stomach felt queasy. She could feel her heart palpitating. Maggie braced herself. She knew what was happening.

The commotion of the marketplace faded to a backdrop as she slipped into a world parallel to the one around her. The fog may have obscured her vision, but this time she held firm as a woman's face dissolved through the whiteout and came into focus like a photograph developing in the print tray. The woman had honey blond hair that fell to her shoulders, the full rounded face of a woman in her thirties, and agate blue eyes that were widened in terror. Maggie felt wobbly on her feet, but wrestled to steady the rangefinder to her eyes. She watched through the camera as the woman tried to scream, but a man's hand quickly covered her mouth. He held her from behind, and dragged her backwards into a textile stall as the woman's arms thrashed about violently, trying to resist him. Maggie could clearly see that a Leica camera was strapped around the woman's neck, swinging back and forth as it bounced across her chest in the struggle. A filigreed archway . . . a blue stucco wall with a crack . . . flashed across the lens. The woman's trembling hand reached out as if begging for someone to take hold of it, then suddenly disappeared behind a wall of darkness.

Maggie bit her lip as she felt herself plummet into a sea of blackness. A drop of blood trickled down her chin. She tried to press the shutter button again, but this time it was stuck. Blue, red, yellow—an explosion of sparks meshed into the patchwork of textiles; their patterns swirling like the menacing eye of a hurricane. The strike of the blacksmith's hammer sounded in the distance. It grew louder as the heat of the sun smoldered on her back. From the square came the faint echo of the *qrakech*, the iron castanets of the Gnawa musicians, signaling the onset of the evening's performance. As the monotonous incantations of trance music began, she locked on to the melody in an attempt to filter out the harsh metallic pounding of the anvil—and then she ran.

This way or that? Panting and out of breath, Maggie limped ahead as fast as she could on her sprained ankle. She remembered the words of Ramos: *"It's easy to get lost . . . you can't go to the souks by yourself . . . it's dangerous for a woman alone."*

A twist, a turn, go right, go left? She felt like a rat in a maze. "The music, follow the music . . ." she repeated to herself. Her mind was still racing when she sensed the presence of a body trailing at her heels. Another hustler, she thought. But when Maggie turned around, she saw that it was the tourist from the American tour bus—the man in the Yankees baseball cap. Was it just coincidence? Or was he actually following her? The chanting of the Gnawa grew louder as the blow of the blacksmith's hammer waned. Maggie knew that she was almost there. She focused on the little girl in Venice who navigated her way out from the winding labyrinth of alleyways. She followed her instincts—and the music that never let her down. The last thing she remembered was staggering towards the Djemaa el Fna and collapsing in a heap of tears.

When Maggie came to, she was once again cradled in the arms of the fortune teller. The plaza was almost empty now, but the Gnawa chorus was still reciting their hypnotic trance music for the few that remained. The old woman massaged Maggie's hands and hummed along as if she were comforting a wounded child. It occurred to her that the woman had murmured a single word on the night of the fire-eater's performance. *"Puzzle,"* she had uttered.

Maggie gazed up from the fortune teller's lap and looked into her face. "Madame, please tell me what you meant by *puzzle*?"

But the woman did not reply.

"S'il vous plait, Madame, what did you mean by a *puzzle*?" Maggie asked again.

But the fortune teller just shook her head.

"My mother," a voice interrupted, "she does not speak much English."

Maggie turned in the direction of the voice. She was astonished to see the chamber maid from the hotel. "But you . . . you can speak English?"

"Yes, so sorry. We are forbidden to speak to hotel guests, but now I can thank you for your concern at my illness. It was very kind of you to notice."

Maggie sat up in attention. The young woman was not wearing a hotel uniform. She was dressed in an eggshell colored caftan and wore a white kerchief on her head. She knelt down beside her on the ground.

"Your mother, she said the word *puzzle* to me. Can you ask her what it meant?"

The young woman addressed her mother in a language that Maggie could not understand. Her mother appeared to mutter something in response, then rocked back and forth to the music.

"Puzzle. She only says *puzzle*."

"But what does that mean?"

"A puzzle, like when two pieces go together," she gestured with her hands, locking her fingers in tandem.

Maggie just sat there in silence. She didn't know what to make of it.

"Please, you must not ask any more questions. It is enough time for you here in Marrakech. You must leave this place."

Why would she tell me to leave, Maggie pondered? "But I can't do that. I have work to do, and I . . ."

The young woman interrupted. "Solve the puzzle that is within yourself—and go home *now!*" she warned.

FOURTEEN

"Ramos, I must speak with you privately. *Please,*" Maggie implored, "is there somewhere we can go?" It was the next morning and Maggie had barely slept all night.

Ramos detected her sense of urgency. He led her to a rooftop café overlooking the square and found a table in a corner where they could have some privacy. "Coffee?" he offered.

"Yes, Espresso, and make it strong. Thanks."

Ramos ordered two coffees and waited for Maggie to compose herself.

She looked him straight in the eyes when she spoke. "Ramos, how did Lily die?"

Ramos shifted in his chair. His body language stiffened.

"Ramos, I need to know. How did Lily die?"

"Maggie, please don't ask this. It is better for you not to ask this."

"It happened in the souks, didn't it?" Her voice became shrill.

"Maggie, lower your voice. No one must hear you."

"I must know! What happened in the textile souk?"

Ramos was taken aback by her knowledge of an incident in the souks. "Alright, alright, I can tell you, but only what you need to know." A worried

61

look crossed his face as he continued. "It was just over a year ago. Lily and Scott were shopping in the souks. Scott was bargaining for some blankets and Lily got impatient. She moved on alone and was browsing through the souks when . . ." He stopped short.

"When what?"

"When she disappeared." His eyes became teary as his voice began to shake. "We searched for her everywhere."

"We? You were there?"

"Yes, I was there. The police shut down the entire marketplace, blocked off all the exits. They searched for days in and out of every souk, but tragically, she was never found."

"Never found? But how do you know she's dead then?"

"She is dead, Maggie. Trust me, she is dead."

Maggie leaned across the table and grasped his hand. "Ramos, I think I know what happened to her. Please come with me to the souk today. Not to photograph textiles, but to find out what happened to Lily."

"No, Maggie, you cannot do this. I beg you."

"Ramos," she pleaded, "if you ever cared for Lily, do this one thing for her. They retrieved her camera, didn't they?"

"How would you know that?"

"My Leica—it's Lily's camera. I bought it at an estate sale in Poulsbo—*Scott's* estate sale. I know it sounds crazy, but I saw Lily through the camera." Maggie retrieved the torn scrap of cloth from her pocket and waved it. "Identify the weave and you locate the tribe that created it. That's what you told me, right?"

Ramos nodded in agreement, but he still didn't understand.

"Lily, she must have stuffed this scrap of fabric into the camera case when she left it behind. Blue triangles interwoven with coral bands. You can trace the origin, can't you?"

"Maggie, there are dozens of shops selling textiles fitting that description in the souk. Please don't do this, it's bigger than you know."

"But Ramos, Lily was leaving us a clue. She was trying to tell us something. If you don't go with me, I'll go alone. Please, I'm begging you," she implored, "do it for Lily."

"Ramos hung his head. The sadness of Lily's loss had been stirred. "Alright," he said, with a sobered inflection she had not heard before. "I'll do it for Lily."

FIFTEEN

Thick pile and flat weave, medallions and diamonds, thin stripes and wide; the vibrant colors of the textile souks exemplified the diverse handiwork of Moroccan and Berber craftsmen. It took an expert to distinguish one particular design from another.

Ramos carried Lily's backpack and led the way. "What makes you think finding this weave pattern will tell us what happened to Lily?"

"Because it's a clue—a clue that she left for us," Maggie insisted.

Ramos examined the scrap of cloth. "This is very different from anything I've seen here. It will be . . . how do you say in America? Like finding a needle in a haystack."

"Wait, there's more . . . I just remembered." Maggie recalled the flickering image of a stucco wall that came to her through the camera. "Through the camera, I saw a stucco wall, blue with a crack split across it. And an arch, a filigreed archway."

"Ramos pointed upwards over their heads. "There's the archway with filigree carvings—it's the entrance to the textile souk."

"Then the wall is the next clue . . . the blue stucco wall."

Maggie and Ramos scanned up and around the roofs, the doors and the broken walls of storefronts. Blue paint, in all its variants of cobalt, aqua and powder, were pervasive throughout the city.

"Distressed and cracking walls are very common in Marrakech—especially blue ones," said Ramos with an exasperated sigh.

Maggie understood his frustration. "But I will recognize *this* wall when I see it. Ramos, I think we need to split up and go in different directions."

"No, Maggie, that's not a good idea," he said. His usually cool disposition was frazzled.

"It's the only way. I promise you that I can take care of myself . . . *really*."

Ramos knew that he could not win. "Alright, alright," he relented, "but, I'll meet you back here, at the entrance, in *one* hour," he said, insistently. "Oh, and Maggie," he added, "keep taking photographs today, so you can upload them to Scott. That way he won't get suspicious."

Maggie wondered why Ramos would be concerned that Scott might get suspicious, but she didn't press him. "Okay, see you back here in an hour."

Now Maggie was on her own again, but this time driven with a confidence that she was on the right track. If she could just relax and follow her intuition, she would instinctively know which way to turn. Maggie grasped the scrap of cloth in her fist and hummed a random melody as she walked along the marketplace. It was the melody of the Gnawa. She pondered if Lily had heard the same music the very night she disappeared. Then there it was. Partially hidden by the layers of fabric draped in front of it was the blue stucco wall. Maggie recognized the crack that broke diagonally in a descent from right to left, and the peel of the paint that exposed the chalky white foundation of the stucco underneath. She flashed on the image of Lily's hand reaching out from a hazy portal.

Maggie approached the entrance to the storefront with some trepidation, then took a deep breath and walked in. A narrow chamber, not more than ten feet across by ten foot deep was dark and poorly lit. The now familiar perfume of orange blossoms and ginger saturated the air. She recognized it as the same scent absorbed by the remnant scrap of cloth stuffed into the camera case. She knew she was in the right place.

Maggie browsed past the tables piled high with folded blankets, rugs, shawls and caftans. Every inch of wall was covered with textiles, but she didn't see anything at all that looked like the weave of Lily's cloth.

"May, I help you, Madame?" Maggie guessed it was the proprietor of the store who stood before her. Light-skinned and of average height, he was dressed in a brown tunic and loose cotton pants. The large black eyes that dominated his rather small face were framed by thick bushy eyebrows, knitted in an expression of curiosity. He glided towards her anticipating her interest. "You like this, maybe?" he held out a yellow embroidered blanket slung over his arm.

"Nice, that's very nice. I'll just keep looking, thank you," Maggie smiled, uneasily. But the souk vendors are known for their persistence.

"Rug, you like a nice rug?" he spoke in a stuttered English, as he peeled back the layers of a neat stack of rugs.

Maggie realized that it was to her advantage to act interested. She gestured to a black and white shawl draped over a hanger. "May I try that on?" she asked.

"Certainly, Madame. A very good choice." He slipped the shawl off its hanger and brought it closer for her inspection. "Notice the fine weave of the pattern."

"Beautiful, it's very beautiful." He came so close that she felt a bit uncomfortable.

"You may try it on—there," he pointed towards the far end of the store where she found a small dressing room hidden behind a curtain. She entered and stood in front of the full-length mirror. What to do next, she sighed. Maggie wrapped the shawl around her shoulders and folded her arms as if fending off a cold chill. A feeling of melancholy washed over her. She felt such a strong bond to Lily. Somehow they were tied together. But this was not only about discovering what happened to Lily. This was also about finding herself.

Maggie examined her face in the mirror. Her eyes looked swollen and red from lack of sleep.

The shawl was very lovely, but she didn't have the heart to buy it. Maggie stepped back to remove it when she noticed the curtain behind her reflected in the mirror. For a moment, she was frozen in her tracks, fixated at the mirror reflection, and unmoving. The pattern of the curtain behind her had blue triangles woven in circles over orange and red bands . . . could it be? Maggie felt her heart thumping in her chest. She spun around and grabbed the curtain. She held it with both hands and scaled the surface from top to bottom. On the lower right corner was a tear! She snatched the scrap of cloth from her pocket and compared the two pieces. The stretched threads, the shredded edges . . . the pattern of the triangles—they matched!

Maggie remembered the night at the square when the young housekeeper attempted to explain her mother's words. "A puzzle. She says you will solve a puzzle . . . like when two pieces fit together." Lily had been here. Lily had been in this very room! The pieces fit!

"She didn't stay here long, Madame." A woman's voice whispered from the other side of the curtain. Maggie turned around, startled to discover the young chamber maid from the hotel standing behind her.

"She wasn't here very here long," she repeated, "only until it was safe to bring her out under dead of night."

Maggie was stunned by what she was seeing and hearing. The chamber maid had evidently been watching her and followed her to the square.

"They were supposed to kill her . . ."

"They?" Maggie interrupted.

But the young woman didn't answer the question and only continued. "Instead, they drugged her with opium and sent her on caravan to the desert. She was sold to a brothel. With her blond hair and blue eyes, it wasn't difficult."

"But then, she's not dead!"

"She is dead."

"But, you said . . ."

"Let it be, Madame. If she is not dead by now, she is surely dead to your world. She can never return. It is done."

The voices of two men in animated conversation filtered into to the dressing room. One of them had an American accent. They drew nearer.

"Madame, you must go now. You are in great danger," said the young woman with fear in her voice. She pressed a hand to the full-length mirror in the dressing room and pushed it. To Maggie's surprise it opened. "Hurry down the staircase and follow the tunnel. It will lead you out of the medina."

A staircase behind the dressing room mirror, a hidden tunnel—but there was no time to ask more questions. She thought she heard a man's voice from inside the store say *"Where is she?"*

"Hurry! You must go, now!" said the young woman. She removed the kerchief from her head and hastily tied it onto Maggie's. "Your hair, you must cover your red hair so they can't recognize you!"

The staircase of concrete steps was maybe only two feet wide and it was dark. Maggie steadied her hands on the wall and descended to the first step, then hesitated. She realized that she never even knew the young woman's name. "May I . . . may I ask your name?"

The woman seemed startled by her question. "My name is Noura," she whispered softly.

Maggie reached out to squeeze her hand. "Thank you, thank you, Noura," she said, her voice breaking into a cry. "And my name is Maggie. I hope we meet again, someday."

Then she turned and ran down the steps.

SIXTEEN

When Maggie emerged from the tunnel, she surfaced in the piles of a junkyard surrounded by heaps of rotting garbage. Her text message must have gotten through because within minutes, Ramos was there.

Ramos extended his arm in assistance. "Let me help you out of this mess."

"Now I know how they got Lily of the medina," said Maggie. "Who would ever think of looking here in this desolate place?" Maggie felt sick to her stomach just thinking about it. She needed to sit down.

A white mini-van and driver waited for them by a chain link fence. They climbed into the back seat compartment and sat there facing each other. When Ramos spoke, it was in a solemn tone. "It's time for you to know the whole story," he said, taking her hands in his. "Scott was running a drug ring through his import business . . . opium . . . hidden in the textile shipments."

Maggie's eyes widened. She was shocked by what she was hearing.

"Lily found out about it. They fought. She was threatening to expose him. He gave the order to have her taken care of—killed."

"Then the kidnapping in the souks was a set-up by Scott?"

"Right, his cronies set it up through third parties, but the plan went wrong. Scott was double-crossed."

"How so?"

"Lily, she was beautiful. They didn't kill her. And the opium shipment, they kept that too."

"And this?" Maggie gripped the scrap of cloth in her fist. "Lily must have stuffed it in the case of the camera she left behind. What does it mean?"

"The shop that you found must have a direct link to the middlemen that Scott is looking for. That must be why your textile photos and my descriptions are so important. One by one, Scott is tracing every textile by region."

"And when he finds the right one, he finds Lily and the people who double-crossed him, right?"

"Right. But Maggie . . ." he hesitated, "you can't go back to the hotel. You must get out of Marrakech. I'm sure Scott never expected you to find out about this. You were supposed to take photographs—that's all. My driver, he'll bring you to Tangier. You can take the ferry across the Straits. My brother will meet you on the other side in Spain—he'll get you back to the States."

Maggie looked him dead in the eyes without flinching. "I promise you that I'll take that ferry to Spain—but not until I find out what happened to Lily."

"It's out of your league, Maggie. This weave is from a nomadic tribe in the Sahara. They move, they change their name. It will be almost impossible to find them."

"What about going to the authorities?"

"The authorities don't have the capacity to infiltrate the tribes. It must be done undercover, and frankly, with a lot of help needed along the way. I promise you that I'll put out some feelers once you're gone. I'll try to find Lily myself, but please, you must go home!"

But Maggie was no longer listening to Ramos. She was looking far away into the distance, past the rotting heaps of garbage to the wider expanse of the remote horizon. Her eyes raced from left to right. Her lips pursed tight. She could no sooner give up on Lily than she could give up on herself.

Was it the stony expression on her face, or the sheer stubbornness of her iron-will that made him shiver?

"I have a plan, and you're going to need me," said Maggie.

SEVENTEEN

It was a four hour drive to Ouarzazate, the desert city just south of the High Atlas Mountains that is the gateway to the Sahara, but it seemed a lot longer. Maggie was feeling a bit carsick from the hairpin turns on the ride up, but didn't dare tell Ramos. She could show no signs of weakness at this point.

From the paved thoroughfares and tree-lined boulevards of Marrakech, they had transitioned to the dusty rock-strewn road of the Tizi n'Tichka Pass where shaves of mountainside, spooned from the recurrent landslides so common to the area, bounced against the tires of their beat-up van.

"We will find better transportation once we get past Ouarzazate," Ramos advised. "But we cannot stay in that area very long. It is a high visibility locale and it could be dangerous for us to be seen there."

Maggie understood. From what she knew of Ouarzazate, it was quite a trendy hotspot, popular with tourists and moviemakers alike. Touted as the "Hollywood of Morocco," Ouarzazate had gained notoriety back in 1962 when its photogenic Kasbah, *Aït Benhaddou*, was chosen as a location for the film *Lawrence of Arabia*. Since then, a string of movies had been made there, giving rise to the souvenir shops and hotels that catered to an influx of sightseers.

But the picturesque city of Ouarzazate had made its mark long before the medium of film had ever been invented. Primarily inhabited by nomadic Berbers who have populated the region for centuries, Ouarzazate once served as a layover for the merchants who journeyed on caravan from Timbuktu to Marrakech, trading slaves, gold and salt. The heritage of the nomadic tribes that once passed this way was diverse; and was reflected in the mélange of faces, language, costumes and crafts that persisted to present day.

Ramos slowed down the van as they drove through city center. Maggie was dazzled by the beauty of the pink city virtually hand-built from the iron-rich clay of the neighboring mountains. The multi-tiered towers of the Kasbah de Taourirt with its huge fortress palace popped against the solid blue of sky, evoking the stately era of its prosperity when in the nineteenth and early twentieth centuries, the Glaoui clan who built it held jurisdiction with the complete endorsement of the French Colonialists. The mountains, the sand, the salmon-colored adobes, and the intermittent appearance of a spired minaret fulfilled her every expectation of a Moroccan desert fantasy.

But there would be no time for sightseeing. Ramos didn't stop the car. "We keep moving," he said. "On to Agdz."

Agdz, an ancient city located approximately fifty kilometers to the southeast of Ouarzazate was formerly a rest-stop on the old caravan route and would serve as the appointed meeting place for their rendezvous with Izri, a family friend of Ramos.

The van whizzed past the outskirts of Ouarzazate. "We can trust Izri. I have known him since I was a child. He will give us supplies, clothes, transportation—and most of all, advice."

Maggie reached over to give Ramos a consoling pat on the shoulder. "How can I ever thank you?" she said. "Thank you for allowing me this crazy plan—and providing me the means to carry it out."

"Don't thank me yet. We don't know if this will work—and I could change my mind at any minute."

Maggie shrunk down in her seat. She knew she was asking a lot of him. "Ramos," she whispered haltingly, "I truly believe that none of this is a coincidence. Every step of the way has led us to this juncture."

Ramos stared straight ahead at the road, gripping the wheel with both hands.

"Think about it. What are the odds that I would walk into an antique store and buy Lily's camera? And then, that my neighbor Joanna would get me a job with Scott—which led me to meeting you? If Lily is still alive, she needs us. We have to know if she is dead or alive, don't we?"

"Yes, we have to know. And it's the only reason that I'm doing this."

But he wasn't happy about it and Maggie could sense it. It felt as if minutes passed before he spoke again.

"If I am honest with myself, I have always wondered what happened to Lily," he began. He breathed a forlorn sigh. "I have never said it out loud . . . but I have felt guilt over this for a long time."

Maggie remained silent, letting him speak.

"I told myself she was dead and never looked any further into it. I didn't interfere. I had a wife and children to think about, I . . ."

Maggie touched his arm gently. "Ramos, you did what you had to do at the time. The important thing is, you are here with me now—and *now* is the right time and place to find out what happened to Lily once and for all."

"But Maggie," he turned to her with that somber expression he sometimes took on. "Don't underestimate the chances we are taking. This is a very dangerous enterprise—and it could all go awry."

When Ramos pulled in to an isolated petrol station in the middle of nowhere, the light of day was already beginning to fade. The unplanned stop awakened Maggie, who had drowsed off.

"Change of plans. Take your backpack and leave everything else behind," he said, clearing out the van and handing the keys off to a young man.

Maggie was confused. Why hadn't Ramos filled up the tank—and where were they going on foot?

"Hurry," he ordered, "we have to cross the river before the sun sets and we lose the light."

Maggie followed at his heels. Cross the river? What river? And how? But there was no time to ask questions. Ramos scrambled ahead and waved her onwards down a steep incline leading to the rocky banks of a river's edge. When she caught up with him, he was waiting with two saddled donkeys beside him.

Maggie was taken aback. "You mean *that's* the new transportation?"

"It is for now. Ever ridden a donkey before?"

"Uh, only once, in Santorini. But that was a long time ago."

"Well then, *once* means you have experience. "Here, I'll help you on."

Maggie approached what appeared to be the more passive of the long-eared burros.

"Don't worry—he's accustomed to strangers," said Ramos, guiding her foot into the stirrup of the saddle. She threw her leg over and held on tight. She knew that donkeys were sure-footed and reliable—much more skillful at crossing a river than any human could be.

Ramos checked his watch. "Izri is waiting for us in Agdz. We'll spend the night there, but it will be a long night. There is much to discuss."

"But why the detour—and why scrap the van?"

"The main road is not secure. Izri sent his nephew to take the van and hide it."

"So he was the man who took the keys at the petrol station, then?"

"Yes, but please, no more questions. There will be plenty of time for questions once we reach Agdz."

When Maggie and Ramos had finally crossed the narrows of the Draa River, the sun had just begun to dip below the desert flats. By cover of darkness, they had managed to avoid the main road while depending upon the trusty footwork of their donkeys to guide the way. It was almost midnight when they arrived at the small Berber village of Agdz where Izri and his wife Tala welcomed them to their home in the foothills of the Djebel Kissane Mountains.

"Bienvenue, mon ami!" Ramos met the open arms of Izri. The men exchanged kisses from left to right in customary European tradition and then hugged each other tightly for several moments. Maggie was touched by their obvious affection for one another.

"My home is your home, my friend," said Izri. "And you must be Maggie," he turned to greet her, smiling warmly.

Maggie immediately saw a resemblance to Ramos. Izri was similarly tall and tan-skinned with a thin mustache and goatee. He was dressed casually in blue jeans and a sweater. She noticed a white djellaba cloak folded on a nearby chair.

"It's so nice to meet you. Thank you for this, for opening your home to us . . . and for helping," she said.

"Well, the name Agdz means 'resting place,' and this is your resting place anytime you need it," said Izri. "Please sit down by the fire and get warm. You must be exhausted from your long journey."

An attractive long-haired woman carried in a tray of tea. "My wife, Tala . . . the mint tea will settle your stomach," said Izri.

Maggie cupped her hands over the glass and let the steam of the hot tea rise to her face. She looked around the room pensively, taking stock of her surroundings. Even in the dim of the lamplight, she couldn't help but notice the striking black carpets of orange-red geometric design that hung from the walls and covered the floor.

Ramos read her mind. "These are traditional textiles of the area—known as Ouazguita," he said. "This is another example of a textile pattern that is identified with a particular region."

"Ah yes, I'm learning," Maggie nodded.

"And these dates are from our garden," said Tala, as she placed a large ceramic bowl on the table. Her long black hair swung loose over her shoulders as she leaned forward. "Please, try some. They will give you back your energy."

In fact, the region was known as the "Date Basket of North Africa" for the prolific date palms irrigated by the nearby Draa River and yielding over eighteen varieties of the fruits.

"Sugar and fiber," said Ramos, as he popped a date into his mouth. "We'll be stocking up on these."

Maggie could feel the elephant in the room. No one wanted to be the first person to broach the subject—what happened outside Ouarzazate and what did it mean? The small-talk ended in an uneasy silence.

"The petrol station . . . what happened?" Maggie blurted.

Izri shot a look at Ramos. Why did she get the impression that Ramos already knew the answer to the question?

"Just a precaution," said Izri.

"It's okay. You can tell me everything," said Maggie. "In fact, it's important that I know everything."

"She's right," said Ramos. "This is her plan and her idea. She needs to know what she is dealing with."

Izri punctuated his words as he spoke. "A business associate of Scott's was sighted in the area. It's possible you were being followed."

For a moment, Maggie flashed back to the American tourist in his baseball cap.

"Don't worry, I'm confident we shook them off," Ramos countered quickly. "But we'll need to watch our back. They're hoping we'll lead them to the people who double-crossed Scott. They'll attempt to trail us—but if we're one step ahead of them, it won't be easy."

Izri pulled his chair alongside Maggie. "That's right, because tomorrow, you will drive to M'hamid, the last oasis before you enter deep into the sub-Sahara desert. You will have supplies, food—and a change of clothes."

It was all part of the plan.

Izri moved closer and spoke in a hushed tone. "My wife Tala, she will show you how to dress in traditional Berber robe and scarf."

Ramos turned to Maggie. "Are you sure you're ready for this?"

"I'm ready," she answered, without hesitation.

"Then from here on, the performance begins."

EIGHTEEN

Ramos cranked the 4x4 into high gear and accelerated on the stretch of open road ahead. "Frankly, no one likes to admit it, but it still exists," he said.

"You mean, the slave trade?" Maggie rolled up the window. The air outside was heating up.

"Human trafficking—young girls, women, sold to the highest bidder. We would like to think this is a thing of the past, a relic of the old caravan merchants who bartered slaves for gold and salt, but . . ."

"But you think it still exists?"

"On some level, yes, I think it does, unfortunately."

"My red hair—it's a novelty here—even more exotic than blond. It should get us multiple offers, yes?"

"I don't know how you talked me into this—but yes—your red hair will draw attention, as it already has. Basically, I am auctioning you off to the highest bidder. This way we move around, we ask questions, and we search the nomadic encampments."

"Looking for the matching textile that will hopefully lead to Lily . . ."

"Yes, looking for the textile pattern—like looking for the missing piece of the puzzle. It's a long shot," he said with exasperation in his voice. "We have no guarantee this will work at all. You could get kidnapped, killed . . . or worse."

Maggie involuntarily let out a nervous chortle. "What's worse than getting killed?"

But Ramos didn't answer and continued to drive on in silence.

Soon, a barren desert of yellow pebbled sand encircled them in all directions; the monotony of its nebulous landscape occasionally morphing into hues of ochre against the glaring sun that had no-thing to block it into shade. Maggie spotted a handful of earthen houses blended in like camouflage against the far range, providing a hint of form to the formlessness of the bland terrain. Many found the desert a place of peace and contemplation, but for Maggie, it was dry and empty and she missed the sea.

"Have yourself one of Tala's dates," suggested Ramos. "It will give you a lift."

Once again, he had anticipated her needs. Maggie retrieved the brown paper bag from the back seat and dug in. "Hmmm . . . delicious." The date was sweet, but not too sweet, and shifted her mood. "Tala is a very wise woman."

"Yes, she certainly is. The void of the desert, it can sap you of your energy, both in body and in spirit."

Maggie downed another fruit. The dates really did perk her up and lightened her disposition. "Must be the sugar rush, eh?"

Ramos paused, "You take it all on yourself, don't you?"

Maggie wasn't sure what he was referring to. "What do you mean—*take it all on myself?*"

"Surroundings, people—they effect you."

"Sure, yes, I guess so." Maggie was a bit unnerved by his comment.

"In the short time I have known you," Ramos continued, "I can see that you are a person who is sensitive to your environment. You pick up on things, you read people."

"I suppose I do, yes."

"Lily, for instance. You have transferred her predicament to yourself."

Maggie was silent. To hear it put that way—it was uncanny. Not even Dr. Caprio had described her situation in those terms.

A series of palm groves signaled the nearness of a metropolis, but Ramos sped right through the township of Zagora. When they had cleared the perimeter of the city and were restored to the stillness of the spartan road, Maggie decided it was time to tell him her story—the *entire* story—of her blackouts, the explosions of color, her stay at the recovery center—she told him everything.

" . . . *Exploding Head Syndrome*—that's the only name I have for it. My doctor tells me it's stress, that it's all in my mind—and yes, it *is* in my mind, but it's so much more than that."

"Well, from everything you've told me, I don't think it's *all* in your mind—and I don't think there is anything supernatural about that camera, either. I think you are an empathic to the extreme."

"An empathic? How so?"

"An empathic—a person who has a knack for tuning in to the thoughts and emotions of others, feels energy, sees beyond surface appearance. An empathic navigates on intuition—in some ways, not unlike the nomads of the desert who follow the currents of the wind. While most people perceive the world through five senses, an extremely empathetic individual may use six or seven. For you, I think this is both a blessing and a curse because when all those sensory perceptions detect great danger, you get locked onto a wave length and your brain goes into overload."

"As in firing too many neurons?"

"Something like that. It's actually amazing how studies in neuroscience are corroborating such experiences."

Maggie had to laugh at the irony of it all. "Maybe I'm going to the wrong kind of doctor then?"

"Yes, perhaps you are," Ramos replied.

Maggie had made her comment in humor, so she was taken by surprise at the serious tone of his response. "So how is it you know so much about this?" she asked.

"Lily, she had such a talent. I think that's why you feel something very strong when you look through the lens of her camera—the same camera her own eyes have looked through."

It was a lot to absorb. "And just what am I supposed to do about this? How do I handle living with this *empathic* thing?"

Ramos answered in a steady and deliberate tone. "Sometimes Lily would get overwhelmed by all the input. She was learning to divert energy when it became necessary. If you can harness those extra senses, you can control your physical reaction. Like with the dates for instance . . ."

"The dates? What do dates have to do with anything?"

"It's just an example. Think about it," said Ramos. "You were engulfed by the dry energy of the desert. It was beginning to have a detrimental effect on you, draining you. When you ate a fruit, you intercepted that unwanted energy and shifted your state."

Maggie thought about it. "I guess so, yes."

"It's a small way to begin—a way to trick your brain, so to speak, by using one of the more accessible of the sensory faculties like taste, smell, touch, seeing, or hearing to divert the focus of energy. You can learn to mobilize your heightened perceptions to your advantage—and with practice, you won't need to eat a piece of fruit or listen to a melody, as you already have often done—instead, you'll do it with your mind."

"Wow, I'm floored by this. I really need to think . . . to think this through."

"Don't think too hard," said Ramos. "That only compounds the problem."

"Yes, yes, of course, you're right." If he only knew how wise he really was, Maggie mused.

Meanwhile, the next great landmark along the road, the pink clay fortress of Tagounite came into view; its spiky rooftops aiming towards the sky. "Enough now, try to relax. Soon we will arrive at M'hamid—and the end of the road."

NINETEEN

When Maggie awakened the next morning in the Kasbah that Ramos had chosen for their overnight stay, her body was still aching from the long car ride. It had been a fitful night and she hadn't slept well at all. M'hamid represented a turning point in their plans and she could feel the anxiety setting in.

At one time a prosperous watering hole on the caravan trail, the small village of M'hamid had for centuries served as a nucleus of exchange between nomadic Berbers and the diverse mix of inhabitants who lived along the banks of the Draa River. More importantly, it lay on the threshold where the mapped road ended and the vast wilderness of the Sahara Desert began. For Maggie, it was the final refuge of certainty before their leap into the unknown. But there was no time for second thoughts now. She knew exactly what she had to do next.

Maggie opened her backpack and unfolded the long white robe that Tala had given her. She slipped into the bulky ankle-length gown and draped the veil of the hood over her head like a kerchief, concealing most of her hair except for a few stray curls. Using a stick of kohl, she applied the thick black liner, a cosmetic customarily used in Morocco, to her upper and lower eyelids and smudged it with her finger. Then, she smeared a dollop of bright red lipstick across her mouth as a finishing touch. Maggie stepped back to examine her face in the mirror. Would this work? She knew it had to.

In the kitchen, Ramos was making final preparations for their departure. He packed cans of food, water, and blankets into large canvas sacks, while two men helped him fold a Bedouin tent into the four-wheel drive vehicle parked out the back door. An elderly woman stirred a pot of cereal on the stove while her young daughter laid out a selection of flatbreads, honey, butter, and plates of olive oil on the table. When Maggie stepped into the room, everyone froze.

It was an awkward moment, but the reaction must have signified that she looked the part she meant to play. Ramos sprinted to her side, breaking the silence. "Don't worry. These are good people—my friends. They understand our circumstances." He poured her a glass of banana milk and offered up a chair. "Please, be seated and eat heartily. We have a long journey ahead."

Maggie remained silent as she crunched on a piece of bread. She was listening carefully to what Ramos had to say next.

"Today, we will enter deep into the Sahara. Our first destination will be the sand dunes of the *Erg Chegaga,* where we set camp for the night. Next day, we ditch the four-wheeler and swap our mode of transportation for camel. We clear the tourist routes and popular sights, and then, we become like nomads. We will literally throw caution to the wind and allow ourselves to become lost in the desert." Ramos paused and then continued with a warning. "This will be the period of time that holds the greatest risk of uncertainty. Basically, we will be placing our destiny in the hands of the unknown." It was the most crucial part of the master plan.

Ramos turned towards the men packing the 4x4 and signaled to one of them. "We will be on our own except for Juba, our Tuareg guide."

Maggie's eyes grew wide as an imposing figure of a man stepped forward. He was a striking presence in his blue indigo robe and headdress. The garments were characteristic of the Tuareg, a semi-nomadic tribe descended from North African Berbers. Frequently referred to as the "Blue Men of the Desert," the Tuareg were easily recognizable by the blue turbans called *tagelmoust* draped about their head and mouth. Dyed in varying shades of indigo, the distinctive headdress was legended to protect against evil spirits, as well as the abrasive desert sands.

Maggie thought him an elegant figure and as he approached, she couldn't help but recall how fitting was the Italian phrase for this first impression—*una bella figura*. His stature was unusually tall and he moved without hurry; his body language possessed of a self-confidence that might otherwise be described as smooth. The whites of his eyes glowed against the brown of his sun-tanned skin; his mouth concealed by the folds of his indigo veil. A long silver sword protruded from his robe.

"Juba, please meet Maggie."

Maggie knew that sharing a name with strangers was not common for the Tuareg, who are protective of their identity at first meeting. She also knew that he would wait for her to speak first.

"Salaam. It's nice to meet you," she finally uttered, feeling severely inadequate at her banal greeting.

"Salaam," Juba responded in a single word, nodding his head in a sign of respect.

"Juba is a loyal and faithful friend," said Ramos. "We can trust him with our lives." Somehow Maggie didn't doubt this for a moment.

"Oh, and one more thing," said Ramos. Beginning today, I need your best game face. I hope you are a good actress because there can be no break in the facade. Even when you are afraid, you must not give yourself away."

"I can do that," Maggie replied, straightening the cowl around her shoulders. "I can do that well."

The implied humor of the sign buoyed Maggie's spirits. "Tombouctou 50 Jours" *(Timbuktu 50 days)* it read. The painting of a caravan of camels indicated the mode of transportation that was partially for the benefit of tourists and partially true to its time, when for centuries merchants paused here on their way to Timbuktu and points unknown.

The sign meant they had officially reached the "Gates of the Desert" at the end of the road in M'hamid and the beginning of nowhere in particular.

An arrow pointed in the direction of the Sahara, but there was no pomp and circumstance as they made their crossing. In fact, Maggie barely noticed as they disappeared into the sands.

"Where one world ends, another begins," whispered Ramos.

TWENTY

Contrary to public perception, the desert is not all sand. Much of the desert is comprised of the scattered rocks the locals call *reg*, or the flat hard earth called *hamada*. But the sand dunes of Erg Chegaga, also known as "The Great Sand Dunes," are the epitome of the classic desert landscape called an *erg* with its sculpted mounds of pure sand reaching a height as great as three hundred meters over a stretch of forty kilometers.

From the gates of M'hamid, they had traversed both *reg* and *hamada*, the stony plains of desert marked with occasional patches of bush, tamarisk and the native acacia tree with its thorny red bark. A brief stop at a watering hole called the Oasis Sacrée (the Sacred Oasis) came as a welcome respite. This cluster of palm trees with its perennial water source served as a fountainhead of survival for the pastoral nomads who came here to quench their herds and replenish their water supplies; debunking another desert myth that an oasis is not necessarily a mirage. But for Maggie, the rest-stop provided more than water—it gave her a first glimpse of the nomadic clans they might encounter along the way—and her first preview of the prowess of Juba.

"When nomads encounter each other in the desert, they size each other up," said Ramos.

"Their dress, their saddles, the way they walk, the way they speak can foretell if they are an enemy or a friend."

It wasn't that Juba really even said or did anything overtly. It was the way he just stood there quietly watching everything. For Maggie, the bands of nomads watering their donkeys, camels and ox-like herds of animals were indistinguishable from each other, but for Juba, every subtle detail held importance. On the surface, it appeared as if he was looking into the distant horizon, but in truth, the penetrating lock of his gaze was taking everything in.

"Juba is doing what comes naturally to him— he is assessing the situation," said Ramos.

The men who led their herds to water's edge wore ordinary clothes as far as Maggie could tell, mostly washed out and colorless, dusted with sand. There were no textiles in sight. A duo of tourists planted themselves in the foreground of the action and posed for photos, using the chaotic scene behind them as a backdrop. Juba signaled to Ramos that it was time to move on.

"This is a popular watering hole, and we are still among sightseers at this point—not likely to find what we're looking for here," said Ramos.

And in fact, no one had even given Maggie a second look.

By the time they reached the grand Erg of Chegaga, the sun had had ample time to cast its shadow over the dips and curves of the morphing landscape as it gently shifted in the wind.

For some reason Maggie had never imagined the desert as moving, but it did move, and it had a surprising dynamic to it in collusion with its partner, the wind. The contours of the hills and valleys were tinted in varying hues of tan, burnt orange and muted yellow, resting upon the whims of an indifferent sun. It was breathtaking to behold, and strangely serene.

Ramos stopped the car and all three sat there in silence for a bit. The silhouette of the off-roader reflected like a mirror across the sands; the profiles of their bodies stretched and distorted in the charcoal black of shadow. If the eerie sight of the Erg Chegaga seemed otherworldly, it may have been because it was. For in fact, the only other place such manifestations of nature could be found were on the planets of Mars and Venus, and the moon of Titan.

Ramos and Juba unloaded the tent and proceeded to secure it with stakes in the sand.

"This spot is as good as any," said Ramos. "There are no trees or boulders or cozy corners to find refuge in anymore—there is only the tent that we carry with us."

The two men moved swiftly with few words spoken between them. The waterproof tent called a *khaima* was made of camel and goat hair and was a style favored by nomadic Berbers for its heartiness and portability. Juba unrolled a soft bed of quilt and spread it over the floor of the tent as ground cover while Ramos hung a patchwork of wool blankets for insulation; their colored textiles reminding Maggie of the reason they were there.

When the tent was completed, all three huddled in the shade of it and waited for the sunset to tear across the sky. From a distance, Maggie could hear the sounds of tam-tam and darbuga drums echoing across the dune fields from another camp, perhaps as invocation to help the night make fall. Juba stoked a fire in the sand and boiled a kettle of water for tea. A scarab beetle grazed Maggie's foot as it scooted by, leaving a zippered set of tracks in its wake. It was a small reminder that the Sahara, even as it deepened, was not devoid of life.

As a spectacular golden sunset began to break, it was reflex for Maggie to reach for a camera, but just as she retrieved Lily's vintage Leica from her backpack, she stopped short of positioning for a shot. This was probably not the best time and place to instigate an EHS event. She let out a soft sigh.

"So when did it begin?" asked Ramos.

"When did *what* begin?"

"The episodes, the Exploding Head Syndrome. There must have been a beginning— something that brought it on."

Maggie traced the edge of the lens with her index finger. She didn't look up. "Yes, you're right. There was a beginning—an initiating event, I suppose you could say, when I was a kid."

Ramos waited for the rest.

"There was an accident . . . my mother—she drowned in a boat accident. I was there. I was with her, but I can't remember what happened. It's all a big white blur." Maggie struggled to continue. Her voice stuck in her throat. "I . . . uh, I was only eight years old at the time—and that's when the syndrome began."

"Perhaps when you have your white-outs, you are returning to that moment—'the big white blur,' as you just described it. Perhaps, you are attempting to invoke a memory in the same way that those tam-tam drums are calling upon the night to come," said Ramos.

"Hmmm, I had never put those two things together before. Maybe that's why I'm drawn to the fog—and the sea. Maybe in a roundabout way, I'm trying to go back there—to that moment where it all began." Her voice was pained as she spoke.

"And that would account for what happens next—the explosions of color in your head. All that energy set in motion to the max—an overload."

The thought of it caused Maggie to squirm. How could all these terrible images come flooding into her mind right now in the spare of the desert? Life was supposed to be simpler in the desert—less things, less clutter, no point of reference to measure or compare—so what were all these stunted memories doing here, anyway?

Juba sat motionless. But he had been listening.

Maggie looked to him with nostalgia. He seemed entirely content to sit there surveying the night—his ears pitched to every sound, his eyes sighted in all directions, his skin responsive to every flap in the breeze. So she was caught entirely unawares when he turned to her and spoke.

"I know who you are," he said.

A chill rose up Maggie's spine. In his plain language, he was probably just trying to say that he understood her, or that he knew where she was coming from—but when he phrased it just that way—well, it stilled her breath.

Maggie looked deep into Juba's eyes and locked in. Somehow he knew her—he *got* her—and she didn't let herself question it any further.

TWENTY-ONE

The wind had been howling all night, slamming against the tent so hard that Maggie thought it might fall right over. When she awakened, she had a headache, her mouth was dry, and her eyes burned with sand. She peeked outside the folds of the khaima to find Juba exchanging words with a Berber man shepherding two large camels by their reins.

An erg was sometimes referred to by locals as a *sand-sea* or a *dune-sea,* and by the looks of the ripples dimpled across the desert floor, it seemed to Maggie that these bynames were quite fitting. For there in the whirling winds of a storm, the surface beneath their feet moved like the fluctuating waters of the sea; and airborne billows of sand twisted and spun like hurricane gales sprinkling into a fuzzy white dust bowl that oddly resembled the fog.

Maggie mounted a camel with Ramos who wrapped his arms around her to grip the saddle. Juba sauntered ahead, leading the way.

"Does Juba know where he's going?" Maggie asked Ramos over her shoulder.

Ramos had a smile in his voice when he answered. "If you ask him, he will say that he does not know."

For the first time Maggie doubted to herself that their plan would work. How would they ever find Lily if they didn't know where they were going and who they were looking for, and with a scrap of cloth as their only clue?

Ramos reassured her. "The Tuareg are known as 'The Blue Wanderers of the Desert' for good reason. They rely on the confidence of their instincts to show them the way. Juba is born from a long line of nomadic tradition—he sees in a way that is hearing—he hears in a way that is seeing. He is sensing his way through. You must have trust, as he does, that the correct circumstances will meet us."

Maggie fixed her eyes on Juba astride his camel. He was poised and unperturbed in his demeanor, meandering across the shifting sands as in a slow rhythmic dance. His blue headdress covered all but his eyes, its tails fluttering behind him in the breeze. "The Blue Wanderers," Maggie muttered to herself . . . indeed, the vast expanse before them suggested a wandering with no direction. There were no paved roads or signposts to show the way anymore. The Sahara that lay ahead was the largest, most expansive desert in the world—and they entered into all eight million square kilometers of it, in blind faith.

TWENTY-TWO

They first appeared as a blurry grey smudge on the horizon—three vague figures grouped together and moving towards them slowly. As the images grew larger, it became apparent that this was a small party of nomadic peoples with their camels. Juba went on alert. He observed their swagger and attitude. Did the camels move spritely as in a freshly made departure, or were they slow and plodding, indicating a long and tiring journey? Were the mannerisms of the riders of young persons or elders? Were the supplies they carried bulky or sparse?

The leader of the approaching party offered the first greeting, speaking in a Berber tongue foreign to Maggie. Juba responded, with Ramos waiting his turn to join in. There was an exchange of words, then all eyes turned to her. Maggie could feel the blood rush to her face. She peeled her eyes downwards to avoid meeting theirs. Was this really happening? She held her breath.

There was a long and agonizing pause before Juba gave the signal to resume their journey. "They are not in the market for a red-haired woman," said Ramos.

The force of the sun was blistering and despite the heat, Maggie secured the heavy veil of her hood over her mouth and nose to protect from the wind-force of the caustic sands. It wasn't long before her bottom hurt from the bumpy ride, compounded by a feeling of nausea that bordered seasickness as the single-humped dromedary switched its gait from left to right in a lopsided fashion. Although she liked to think she had a high tolerance for such bone-shaking irritations, this was getting to her.

Little did Maggie know but that like countless nomadic journeyers before her, she had entered unto the *tenere*, the occurrence of unmarked space that is a borderless expanse representing both a physical and mental challenge. Not only did she feel hot, and dry and achy, but she longed for the familiar signs of home again. Lost in the emptiness of the *tenere*, she was experiencing *asuf*, a term coined by the Tamãshaq nomads to characterize the aura of "homesickness" that the journeyer feels at the separation from everything they have ever known.

Indeed, the deeper they penetrated the *tenere* of the Sahara, the more the homesickness of *asuf* crept in. Maggie recollected what Ramos had told her on the road to M'hamid: *"The void of the desert, it can sap you of your energy, both in body and in spirit."* She realized that she needed to shift her mood, but this time Tala's sweet dates were not at hand.

"With practice, you won't need to eat a piece of fruit or listen to a melody—you'll do it with your mind," the words of Ramos resounded.

Maggie closed her eyes and tried to imagine the quaint streets of Poulsbo, her adopted hometown on the shores of the Kitsap Peninsula. She saw herself raising the blinds of the big bay window of her new apartment overlooking the harbor where sailboats drifted over the dark blue waters of Liberty Bay. She felt the cool moist air of the sea breeze brush against her face. She heard the squawking of an impatient pelican waiting for some stray bait to fall from a fishermen's line. Soon, the windswept sands of the dune-sea transformed into a sea of waters, and the wobbling to and fro of the camel became the rocking of a ship.

When she opened her eyes, the sand storm had escalated, permeating her vision like a mist. The brutal power of the wind rapped against her body, forcing her to cower at its repeated thrashings. She could feel Ramos behind her, holding tight at her back, but she could barely see Juba, just a few feet ahead. The camels carried on, as was their nature—and this time, so did she. For a sense of tranquility had washed over her and the daunting willfulness of the desert could bind her spirit no more. Imagining herself in Poulsbo had refreshed her state of mind and remedied the melancholy of *asuf*. She felt peaceful and centered in the midst of the turmoil around her. She had found the stillness in the eye of the storm.

TWENTY-THREE

Would they turn and fade away? Would one leave and another come forward? Maggie found herself questioning if she was seeing a mirage. For as the ending of the storm settled its dust into benign wisps of feathery air, she spotted two groups of peoples at the skyline. Juba sat upright, clutching his sword. She knew this meant he *felt* something.

One group approached from the East, and the other from the West. Both drew nearer, separate and apart from each other, yet each group headed in their direction. Juba arched his back in a show of power. He was on guard.

"Just keep still, and don't say a word," Ramos warned. His voice was rigid.

Maggie observed as the group from the East arrived first—three men and two women on camels, leading a donkey piled high with blankets, most probably for trade. They stopped in their tracks at about a distance of twenty feet or so, and waited for a greeting. But Juba remained silent until the next group arrived.

The clan of people coming from the West moved more slowly, perhaps indicating a longer and more tiring journey. They traveled in a string of five camels sporting red braided threads on their mouthpieces and leather-stitched saddles on their backs. Satchels of what were either merchandise or supplies hung from their sides. There were five men and three women in the caravan.

Juba gave the first greeting, "Salaam," and carefully nodded his head towards neutral ground down the middle of the two groups. Maggie could discern by their colors that the two clans were separate tribes from different regions.

The group from the West was more colorful, even garish. Their women were adorned in a patchwork of patterns: green and purple stripes, yellow and red chevrons, blue and black triangles of wide weave and tight weave; so many in their variety that Maggie could not distinguish one from the other.

The group from the East was more modest in their display. Their three camels were unadorned and the women's clothing was less distinct, woven of simple but fine stripes.

Juba cued Ramos to bring his camel forward and indicated it was time for him to speak. Once again, Ramos conversed in a Berber language, addressing the clans simultaneously and making certain to treat them equally. Then suddenly—he reached down and yanked the hood off Maggie's head. Her red curls released to view, falling over her forehead and onto her shoulders. He parted her hair to reveal her face. For the first time, Maggie felt true terror at the prospect of what was about to happen.

Ramos proceeded to dismount the camel and led Maggie to her feet. She stood there as members of the two tribes came forward to scrutinize her, and in a moment she was surrounded. Juba did not move from his position.

What appeared to be the leader from the Western, more affluent group retrieved a pouch from the sleeve of his robe and shook out the contents in the palm of his hand, revealing three gold nuggets. It was an offer. But Ramos kept a poker face and turned toward the group from the East. The leader from the Eastern troupe counted out first one, then two, then three gold nuggets to match his rival's proffer. A bidding war had begun.

Words flew from East to West and the dialogue became animated. The elder from the Western group was the more aggressive, gesticulating with his hands and arguing with his men about what to do next. Maggie could only interpret that they were haggling over the price. The man stepped closer, addressing Ramos in a hushed and persuasive tone. Then he opened his hand to reveal a fourth gold nugget in his open palm. The group from the East did not counter.

Was this it? Was this the winning offer? Maggie stole a glance at Ramos, but his face revealed nothing. It looked as though the leader from the Western troupe had won the bid, but Maggie got a bad feeling. The man circled around her pacing, and coming so close that she could almost hear him breathing. He paused and then pointed to her robe. Did he want to see more before he closed the deal? Maggie began to shiver. She was about to break down.

Until this point, the Berber women had remained ambiguous figures in the background, deferring to the actions of their men, but now, one of them unexpectedly came to her aid. Grabbing a blanket off the back of a donkey, a Berber woman from the Eastern troupe rushed to Maggie's side and wrapped the blanket around her; shrouding the length of her body in a protective cloak. Maggie buried her face in the folds of the blanket and began to weep. The woman kept a steady arm across her shoulder, consoling her with a caress. For moments, no one spoke or moved.

The gesture of the Berber woman who had stepped out of her place in an act of kindness was brave, if not defiant; her deed of compassion stirring Maggie to remember that courage was the other side of fear. As she choked back her sobs and lifted her head to say thank you, her eye caught a glimmer of color that prompted her to look down at the blanket swathed around her. It had a coral red weave with a pattern of cobalt-blue triangles woven in circles. Her mind flashed back to the scrap of fabric left behind by Lily—it was a match!

A surge of electricity pulsated up her spine. Maggie looked over at Ramos in an attempt to communicate. She knew she had to get his attention and stop him from closing the deal for four gold nuggets with the group from the West.

Instinctively, she lifted the blanket and steadily fanned it out in her arms as if to drape it over her head. Ramos did a double-take at her exaggerated display. He knew it meant something. Maggie stared deep into his eyes and then down at the blanket. She gave the slightest nod that would only have been detected by him. He got the message—it was the color and weave of the textile they were looking for!

The elder from the Western group was gloating in the victory of his winning bid, but somehow Ramos would have to interject and reverse the outcome. He turned to Juba, who all this time had been seated on his camel, quietly observing all that transpired.

Then suddenly, Juba spoke: "The saddle from the East," he said, pointing to a wooden saddle on the lead camel belonging to the Eastern troupe. "This is a very fine saddle."

Ramos had his out. Three gold nuggets and the wooden saddle would shift the favorable result to the Eastern tribe and could not be challenged. He made his trade.

Maggie let out a sigh of relief—but the relief didn't last long. As the three women of the Eastern clan took her into their charge, she realized that she didn't have a plan. With so much emphasis placed on finding the right textile, she and Ramos had never discussed what would happen from here on out.

As the women led her away, Maggie looked to Juba and thought she saw him move his lips.

Although he never said the words out loud, she was certain he mouthed: "I will find you."

TWENTY-FOUR

The encampment was a circle of nine tents pitched in the style of nomadic travelers who moved from place to place. Nearby, were the remnants of an old outpost, perhaps a former oasis that had since been depleted of its water source.

The three women from the caravan escorted Maggie to the larger of the buildings, a crumbling adobe structure topped with a clapboard roof. They gave her a hot bath, dressed her in warm clothes, and brought her a plate of couscous and vegetables for a meal. Then they closed the door behind them and locked it.

Maggie surveyed the contents of the windowless room—a small table, a single chair and a mattress on the ground. An assemblage of blankets were hung from the walls and a stockpile of assorted carpets were stored in a corner. An oil lamp provided the only light.

What to do now? It was the only thing she could think of. Maggie reached for her knapsack and dug to the bottom, retrieving Lily's camera. She held it in her hands.

"Lily, are you here? Where are you, Lily?" she whispered under her breath. But no answer came to her.

She raised the camera to her eyes and looked through the viewfinder, zooming in on the blankets draping the walls, predominantly woven with the now familiar coral threads and blue triangles. "Lily . . . Lily . . . Lily," she chanted repeatedly. But this time, there were no fireworks or visions.

Maggie heaved a deep sigh of frustration from the depth of her gut, swallowing a gulp of air, then exhaling so hard that her mouth quivered. But the sound she heard was not her own—or was it? She sat up to attention and focused her ear. Had she heard a groan—or was she imagining it?

Her instincts told her the camera was key. Using the lens as a magnifier, Maggie scoured the details of the walls that surrounded her for a second time. Closer, then closer still, she zoomed in tighter until she could see every minor feature of the cobalt blue triangles and coral red weave that was the textile design she had pursued across the desert. She noted that the triangles were sometimes uneven and crooked; their imperfections common to the hallmark of an authentic handicraft. The coral striped backdrop was alternately faded and ruddy, indicative of the dye cast and desert sun.

It was something she would normally have dismissed as entirely ordinary, but now she doubled back to take another look. Between one spot in the overlap of blankets that smothered the walls from ceiling to floor was a small black gap reflecting a shadow—enough of a shadow that it betrayed a distance from the wall behind it. Could it be that these layers of fabric were just a façade? Maggie shot up from the chair and zeroed in on the breach of space where she discovered the blankets were at least four deep; and overlapping each other in turns like detours on an obstacle course. One at a time, she flipped their edges and slid herself through until she reached what felt to be the rear wall. Laying her palms flat to the surface, she probed in all directions, using her fingers to see in the dark. She touched upon an object that felt like a latch—and when she turned it, it opened. Yes! There was a door—a hidden door concealed behind the camouflage of textiles.

Pushing it open revealed another chamber, but it was dark and she could barely see. Maggie ran back to the table and grabbed the oil lantern. "Lily? Lily, are you there?"

As she entered the room, a veil of smoke obscured her view. She coughed to clear her throat, and heard another sound. This time she was certain it was not her own, and she followed it.

Was this a dream, or was this a mirage? For there, in the middle of the Sahara Desert was the sight of a European canopy bed with an ornately carved mahogany frame and headboard. A curtain of translucent French tulle was tied to each of the four bedposts with gold braided cords, and a broken chandelier dangled from the ceiling like a prop on a movie set.

Lying on a coverlet of plush satin sheets was a blonde-haired woman dressed in an ivory lace slip. The woman was curled up on her side in a fetal position and appeared to be heavily drugged. Her head was propped with white fur cushions and she whimpered softly, maybe delirious. Maggie knew immediately that it was Lily. She was alive!

"Lily, Lily, it's me Maggie," she cried, almost expecting that Lily would know who she was. The woman did not look well. Her face was ashen and her frame was slight, maybe for lack of nourishment.

"Lily, can you stand up?"

But the woman did not respond.

Maggie recalled the words of Noura in the textile souk; and those of Ramos on the car ride to Agdz. *"If she is not dead, she is dead to this world,"* they had said. But Maggie refused to believe it.

Outside, a commotion ensued. Maggie could hear of the voices of an argument taking place. Two of the men spoke in English and had American accents. She guessed they were Scott's accomplices, having followed her trail to the camp.

"You have two choices—either the shipment or the money," she heard one of the men say. She knew their first order of business would be the double-cross on the opium shipment, but she had to get out before they came for Lily next.

"Lily, please, I need you to stand up," Maggie pleaded. She lifted Lily's arm over her shoulder and leveraged her body as best she could; half dragging, half carrying her to the one small window she could find. Then, with all the force she could muster, she wiggled the rusty iron bars from their screws and pushed them out. She was running on pure adrenalin now.

"Bam!" There was a loud crash outside. The argument outside grew louder and angrier. It sounded as if blows were being exchanged as the altercation between the men turned physical. Maggie used the distraction of the brawl to cover her jump from the window, hauling a non-responsive Lily behind her.

Clutching Lily, frozen in her arms, Maggie crouched beneath the window to hide from view. She could hear the banter of Scott's men entering the chamber and knew it would only be a matter of seconds before they were discovered. She held her breath. She had no plan and no strategy. There was only the moment at hand.

"Out there! Outside!" The men spotted them below the open window, but the window was a narrow one and the men were unable to climb through it. They backtracked to the front door, giving her and Lily some lead time to escape. But escape to where?

The night was dark and indistinct of form, the sand-sea merging into a pitch of blackness with no directional indicators from north to south, or east to west. To Maggie, it all looked the same, but there was no time to stop and think about it—instinct told her to *run*.

"Lily, please wake up—I need you to run with me," she begged. But Lily's body was limp and her eyes did not meet hers.

Maggie scanned the night sky with its sparkling stars and wished for Juba, who always seemed to know what to do next. Then she remembered the words of Ramos: *"If you ask him where he is going, he will say that he does not know."*

"Just *go*, and the rest will come," she told herself. With a physical strength she had never known herself capable of before, she leveraged the weight of Lily's body over her hip and shoulder and ran into the blackness of night without regard to direction. If Scott's men were chasing her, she never looked behind her to check. She blocked out all sounds of them and only focused straight ahead.

She ran, and ran until a swash of blue light became visible in the distance. She aimed towards it like a lifeline until it grew in intensity. And then she realized that it wasn't a blue light at all—it was Juba in his indigo robe and with sword drawn. He had found her—just as he said he would.

Together they ran to where Ramos waited behind the wheel of a 4x4. Juba piled Maggie and Lily into the backseat of the car and covered them with blankets. Then, they drove as fast as they could.

"We head for Tangier now!" shouted Ramos. They were not safe until they could cross the Straits of Gibraltar to Spain.

TWENTY-FIVE

All the signs were there—the clouds, the rain, the cool air—the *Viento de Levante* was setting upon them. Known for its gale force winds inciting turbulent currents and thick murky fog, the winds of the Levante, a Spanish term for strong eastern winds, notoriously swelled to their greatest intensity through the narrow passage of the Straits of Gibraltar from Morocco to Spain.

When Maggie emerged from back seat of the car, a blast of cold air hit her face, perhaps the portend of things to come. "Quickly, we must move fast," ordered Ramos, ushering Maggie and Lily to the dock where a motorboat awaited them.

Maggie noticed Ramos pass an awestruck gaze at Lily. With all that had transpired, he had barely had time to absorb the magnitude of seeing her once again. As he helped a defenseless Lily step onto the boat, the posture of his body softened into a vulnerability only equaled by her own fragility. He cupped Lily's face in hands. "It's really you," he whispered, as his eyes filled with tears of gratefulness. Then shaking himself free of emotion, he snapped back to the urgencies at hand.

"We must leave without delay," he said. "Scott's men cannot be far behind and the fog is rolling in."

118

But Maggie stood fixed at the edge of the dock and waited for Juba.

"He is not coming with us," said Ramos. "His home is here."

Maggie was taken aback. If Juba was not coming with them to Spain, then this was the last time she would ever see him. How could she say goodbye to this person who had touched her life so deeply? Maggie stood there motionless as Juba walked towards her. The whites of his eyes glowed against the tan of his skin, just as the first time she met him; and his blue headdress was ever more radiant against the dreary grey docks of the port.

"I will never forget you," she voiced. But Juba raised his index finger in a gesture that indicated she not speak. The veil over his mouth dropped to his chest, revealing his parted lips that hinted at the slightest of smiles. Maggie understood. Just as they had always understood each other without words spoken. For mere language was inadequate to their communication. Mere words would only get in the way. She took a long and lasting look at Juba—and he at her. *"I will find you,"* she recalled he had mouthed in the unbounded terrain of the desert landscape. And somehow, she knew that they could find each other's presence at any time and any place, wherever in the world they might be. She would never have to say goodbye.

As Ramos geared up the motor for departure, Maggie took a seat in the boat and sheltered Lily in her arms. Juba stood tall, and as if on watch, he

119

held his hand to his sword until their boat disappeared into a cloud of fog.

The Strait of Gibraltar is a narrow channel of waters about fifteen kilometers wide and fifty-five kilometers long, serving as a liaison between Morocco and Spain. Skirted by land masses rising thousands of feet high on either side, an unstable wind tunnel is created when the conditions of the Levante set in.

Maggie held on tight as tempestuous flights of wind kicked up a rough surf of wave activity; relentlessly pounding the boat and rocking it like a seesaw. A whiteout of fog suffused the atmosphere making it impossible to navigate the fishing boats and ferries that crowded the passageway along with theirs. Making a bad situation worse, they knew they would be suspect to the Coast Guard by virtue of their motorboat, the vehicle of choice for illegal immigration that would be tracked for its speed and unpredictability. But there was no way they could let themselves be turned back now.

"Whoosh!" A small fishing boat came dangerously close to theirs, almost sideswiping them. "I cannot see a thing in this damned fog!" yelled Ramos. Maggie's stomach tied up in knots at the close call. Lily lay in her lap, lifeless and unawares.

The blare of a foghorn sounded in the distance, giving Maggie an eerie reminder of her childhood flashbacks. She gripped the sides of the boat and held on tight.

"Vroom!" Another boat came perilously close, but this time, it could not have been a mishap. This was a powerboat and this was intentional. The voices coming off the bow were shouting in English: "It's the end of line. We've got you this time!"

Maggie recognized the man in the baseball cap at the helm. Scott's men had finally caught up with them. Ramos accelerated and cut a thirty degree turn. Behind them, a ferryboat filled with passengers sounded its horn for a second time as it drew dangerously close. Scott's men circled and readied for another swipe, attempting to topple them into its direct path. Ramos had to correct his course *now* before the ship came any closer.

"Bam!" They had been broadsided. Ramos hit the controls and tried to unjam their position but they were stuck and the ferry was headed right towards them.

"Maggie—the flare! Get the flare from the emergency box—there at the bottom of the boat!"

Maggie fumbled, half-blinded by the fog and rain. Crawling on her knees, she felt her way to the bottom of the boat and recovered the flare.

"Pull off the cap and strike it! Strike it like a match!" Ramos shouted as the ferry came closer.

Maggie pulled the cap and struck the tip of the flare. A burst of light shot high into the air cascading red and yellow sparks from its tail. The captain of the ferryboat acted to revise his course, but it was too late. Caught in the turbulence of the ferry's path, the motorboat rolled over, hurling them into the dark murky waters of the straits.

Maggie clutched onto the hull of the boat. The cloud of the Levante was a complete white-out. She could see nothing. "Lily, Lily, where are you?" she screamed. Ramos was nowhere to be seen.

The blast of sound began with the familiar metallic noise that clamored like a cymbal in her head. A foghorn sounded as the sea smoke grew thicker around her. Maggie thought she saw a woman's face coming towards her through the haze, but she wasn't sure. "Lily, is that you?" The image of a hand pierced through the fog and stretched its fingers towards her. She felt her heart pounding through her chest.

Maggie threw one leg over the back of the boat and hoisted herself up. "Take my hand!" If only she could grab onto her, she could pull her back onto the boat and they could both be saved.

The world turned to blackness in an explosion of blue sparks, then red, yellow and green like an aurora of fireworks shooting in all directions—like the fire eater's torch—like the trail of the flare gun. But it wasn't Lily's face she saw this time. It was her mothers.

Suddenly, she was eight years old again, sailing with her mother when the boat toppled over and they fell into the sea. Maggie had managed to climb onto the capsized hull and believing she could save her mother, she extended her tiny hand to rescue her. *"Take my hand, take my hand,"* she had pleaded, stretching out her short fingers until her mother managed to grip them. But she was just a child and could not have known that she was much too small and not nearly strong enough to take on such a feat.

Just as on this night, a foghorn sounded as a ferryboat drew nearer, causing waves of turbulence that loosened her hold. Little Maggie felt her small fingers slip, and her mother's hand let go, disappearing into the fog forever.

"Maggie—over here!" It was the voice of Ramos. He was swimming towards the boat floating Lily at his side. Maggie reached out her hand to meet Lily's. She was not a child of eight years old anymore. This time, she could do it. With all her strength, she clung to Lily's hand and did not let go. For the first time, Lily showed signs she had awakened from her stupor. Gasping for the breath to live again, she looked straight into Maggie's eyes as she was lifted to safety.

All at once, the floodlights of the Coast Guard deluged the waters. The jarring sounds of a helicopter cut overhead.

"FBI, Interpol, you're under arrest," yelled a voice on loudspeaker. And the two men working for Scott were taken into custody.

TWENTY-SIX

It was just a formality but it had to be done. At the Police Station in Poulsbo, Maggie and Ramos sat positioned behind a two-way mirror in a darkened room arranged specifically for witness identification. Six men paraded by in succession and stood before them, first full frontal and then in profile. Maggie recognized Scott from the moment he walked in. He was second from the left in the police lineup.

This time, he was not reminiscent of a swashbuckling Errol Flynn, but he *was* perhaps a lady-killer of sorts—a smuggler, a thief, and an attempted murderer. His thick black hair no longer fell in a debonair wave over his forehead, but was slicked back and matted, revealing traces of a receding hairline that she had not noticed before. The thin tapered mustache that once framed his dimpled smile was now drooped at the edges in a frown. Maggie hoped he could guess it was her behind the glass window and she lingered for a bit as he stood there waiting meekly.

"That's him," she said. "Second from the left."

"Are you sure?" asked the FBI investigator.

"Absolutely sure," Maggie answered, never breaking her fix on Scott as he stood against the wall.

"I can corroborate that," said Ramos. "I have known him for years."

The FBI official opened a loose-leaf book of photographs and placed it before Maggie. "And these women, do you recognize any of them to be Joanna Mills, your neighbor?"

It wasn't difficult to identity Joanna with her pageboy hairdo. "So Joanna turned out to be Scott's conspirator then?"

The agent confirmed Joanna's role. "Conspirator, business partner, and girlfriend. We've been watching Scott and Joanna for a long time now. We suspected Scott was smuggling more than textiles right from the start and we became suspicious when his wife Lily disappeared for dead."

If the FBI investigator leaning over the table looked oddly familiar, it was because Maggie had seen him before. It all fell into place now. No more the scrappy blond hair and embroidered jumpsuit, she barely recognized him out of context.

"Lars, the Norwegian farmer stationed outside Grimwald's Antique Store—it was *you!*"

"Special Agent, J.T. Ballard, FBI. I was undercover in Poulsbo for the last year. Sorry, but of course I couldn't tell you that at the time."

"I have to say that you really did give me the creeps standing there like a statue with a pitchfork." She had to laugh when thinking back at her reaction. "Was there anyone else involved that I should know about?" Maggie could only

125

wonder what astounding news would be revealed next.

Ballard pressed a buzzer to speak on the intercom. "Max, come on in."

A handsome young man entered the room and offered his hand. He had long blond hair and beamed a toothy white smile.

Maggie hesitated. She couldn't place him.

"Best chowder in town!' he said.

"Don't tell me—Johann, the waiter at the Norse Harbor Restaurant?"

"The very same."

Maggie shook her head in disbelief. This was a lot to soak in. She thought back to the moment when she had tried to read "Johann's" lips as he whispered in the ear of the hostess.

"Well, it's nice to know that the good guys were looking out for me," she smiled.

"We surely were Miss Bran. At all times, we surely were."

"And there was someone else looking out for you too," Ballard chimed in.

When the door opened for a second time, it took Maggie's breath away. Standing there was Brett, her ex husband.

"When Joanna solicited your photography services for Scott, we contacted Brett. We wanted to be sure we knew everything about you and were able to track you at all times."

Maggie gaped at Brett in amazement of what she was hearing. "That day at Scott's office—you were there on the boardwalk when I came out—

looking at some real estate, you said."

"It was the only excuse I could think of at the time," said Brett sheepishly. He fidgeted as he dug his hands into the pockets of his bomber jacket. "I could never let anything bad happen to you. I could never give up on you."

Those were the words she had longed to hear.

Ramos had only three more days left in Poulsbo and Maggie was determined to make the most of it.

"Let's go," said Maggie, "I have so much to show you."

She held out one hand for Brett and another for Ramos. Together they walked past the hand-painted storefronts of Poulsbo at a quickened pace, more from excitement than from a rush to get anywhere in particular.

"Look there!" said Maggie. "It's Grimwald's Antique Store."

"And there—Mrs. Olsen's bakery! Let's pick up some pastries for Lily."

Not merely the facsimile of a time gone by, nor the pretense of a faux veneer, the town coined "Little Norway" was so much more than it appeared to be.

AFTERWORD

Accounts of "Exploding Head Syndrome," also known as "Exploding Brain Syndrome," can be found in chat rooms and discussion boards across the Worldwide Web.

Researchers in the field of Cognitive Neuroscience continue to gain new perspectives on the mysteries of the brain and how we perceive reality.

www.ingramcontent.com/pod-product-compliance
Lightning Source LLC
Chambersburg PA
CBHW072357190626
46811CB00019B/1122